MEET THE GIRL TALK CHARACTERS

Sabrina Wells is petite, with curly auburn hair, sparkling hazel eyes, and a bubbly personality. Sabrina loves magazines, shopping, sleepovers, and most of all, she loves talking to her best friends.

Katie Campbell is a straight-A student and super athlete. With her blond hair, blue eyes, and matching clothes, she's everyone's idea of Little Miss Perfect. But Katie has a few surprises for everyone, including herself!

Randy Zak has just moved to Acorn Falls from New York City, and is she ever cool! With her radical spiked haircut and her hip New York clothes, Randy teaches everyone just how much fun it is to be different.

Allison Cloud is a Native American Indian. Allison's supersmart and really beautiful. But she has one major problem: She's thirteen years old, five foot seven, and still growing!

HORSE FEVER

By L. E. Blair

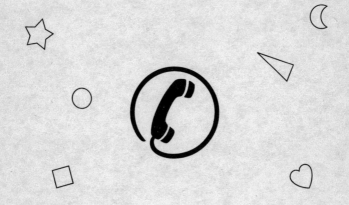

GIRL TALK® series created by Western Publishing Company, Inc.

Western Publishing Company, Inc., Racine, Wisconsin 53404

Text by Katherine Applegate

Chapter One

"Watch this," I said, winking at my friends. "I'm going to fly."

We were walking through town together after school on Wednesday afternoon, and I thought they could use a little excitement.

"Here goes." I threw my skateboard down on the sidewalk and hopped on. With a couple of good, hard kicks, I built up some speed and headed straight for the low wooden bench. The benches were installed a few weeks ago at bus stops around town by the Acorn Falls city council. A great idea, I thought — for reasons of my own.

"Randy! Look out for that bench!" Sabrina Wells cried.

Of course I saw the bench. I was aiming straight for it. At the last minute, just before my knees would have slammed into it, I jumped straight up, tucking up both my legs. My board sailed under the bench and I flew over it. A second

1

later I landed back on the board. I wobbled a little, but stayed on and kept rolling.

I took a sharp turn and headed back to my three best friends. They were staring at me with their mouths wide open. "I call it the 'Zak Attack Air' move," I said, grinning. "You like?"

"Randy Zak, you scared me to death!" Sabs said, fanning her face with her hand like she was going to faint or something.

"Nice move, Ran," Katie Campbell said with a nod. Katie wasn't awestruck, like Sabs, but I did appreciate her compliment. Katie is a hockey player — on the *boys'* team — and hockey players make all kinds of crazy moves on their skates.

To look at Katie, you'd never imagine her gliding around a hockey rink, getting roughed up and out of control. She's totally preppie, with perfect, long straight blond hair, and always wears socks that match her sweaters. But Katie, a very determined kind of person. Once she sets her mind on something, she's hard to stop.

"You must have practiced that trick for months," Sabs said.

"Not that long," I replied. "Only since they put in the benches. I could almost do it with my eyes closed. Want to see?" Of course, I wasn't actually going to do it with my eyes closed. I'm not *crazy*.

"Don't you dare, Randy," Sabs said. "I knew a boy once, or at least my brother knew him and he told me all about him, who used to do all kinds of tricks on his bike and he was really good, they even had him on the TV news once, and he was jumping off a ramp and trying to go over an old junky car and he missed and broke his leg. Or maybe it was his arm."

Naturally, Sabs managed to say all that in one breath, without stopping. She is truly amazing. Not just because she can talk a mile a minute, but because she is the most enthusiastic person in the world. It is almost impossible to be bummed out around Sabs. She's tiny, not even five feet tall, but it's like she's this five-foot-tall light bulb with curly red hair, if you know what I mean.

"Well, I won't break my leg. Or even my arm," I reassured Sabs. "Although I will admit I did get a few bumps and bruises perfecting my technique."

"But why do it at all when you know you could get hurt?" Sabs asked.

"She just loves living life on the edge," Allison Cloud teased. Allison knows me better than anyone else in the world, except for my mom and my

3

friend Sheck, who lives in New York. Al's actually a full-blooded Native American Indian. She's tall and exotic-looking, with big dark eyes and shiny black hair. She was offered a modeling contract once, and she even made a clothes commercial a while ago for my dad, who's a producer. But Al would much rather read a good book than stand in front of a camera for hours.

"Hey, when I lived in New York City, just walking down the street could be an adventure." I said, laughing. "The biggest thing to worry about here in Acorn Falls is that you'll fall asleep in class and get detention."

See, I moved to Acorn Falls, Minnesota, with my mom when she and my dad got divorced. At first I thought my life was over. I mean, *Acorn Falls*? Not exactly the home office of excitement. We got here at the beginning of the school year, and I wanted to move back to New York City worse than anything in the world. But then I met Sabs and Katie and Al at Bradley Junior High School, and things started to change. To my amazement, I actually began to *like* it here.

"Hey, let's get going, guys," Al said, "or all the tables at Fitzie's will be taken. That is, if Fitzie's is exciting enough for you, Randy!"

"Maybe she could skateboard over the tables," Katie offered.

"Or leap the deep fryer," Sabs said.

I shook my head. "If I wanted to be really daring, I'd try eating one of Fitzie's burgers."

Allison slapped her hand to her head in mock horror. "No one is *that* brave!"

When we got to Fitzie's, it was packed. Our regular booth near the back was filled, so we grabbed the first empty one we saw by the front door.

Fitzie's is our after-school hangout. Most afternoons every person there is from either the junior high, like us, or the high school. It's this cool, kind of old-looking place, with a certain style all its own. When I lived in New York, there were about a million different restaurants, but I don't remember any like Fitzie's, the kind of place where you can just hang out every day. There are some nice things about life in a small town, I guess.

A waitress came by and took our order. Katie and Al started talking about a homework assignment for English. I was sitting right across from Sabs, so I was the first to notice that she had something strange sticking out of her hair.

"What's this?" I leaned over and plucked a

white card out of her curls. "Bike for Sale?" I read out loud, making everyone laugh.

"What?" Sabrina lifted her hands to her hair. "Hey — here's another one!" She reached down the back of her jacket collar and pulled out a slip of yellow paper. "Reliable baby-sitter. Reasonable rates."

By now we were laughing pretty hard. "Maybe it's that new shampoo you bought?" Allison teased.

"Maybe it's that weird disease we learned about in health class," Sabrina replied good naturedly. "Bulletin board head."

Just then a big group of kids came in, and our table was suddenly showered with even more signs.

There was a bulletin board on the wall behind Sabs and Katie, and every time the door opened, the breeze was blowing the signs off.

"Oh, now I get it." Sabs turned and looked up at the bulletin board on the wall behind her, which was covered with posters and advertisements.

"I always wondered why this table is the last one to get filled," Al said, piling up a few of the papers that had landed on our table. "I guess I know why, now."

"Here, just hand me all that stuff," Katie said. She turned around and knelt on the seat, so she could reach the board. I'll just grab some of these thumbtacks and stick it back up."

"I'll help," Sabs said, doing the same. Al and I handed them the pile of papers.

"Hey — wait a minute, guys!" Sabs said excitedly. She bounced on the seat cushion, holding up a printed sheet of blue paper. "Listen to this! It's from Rolling Hills Stables."

"Boy, it must be an old ad," Katie remarked. "They've been out of business for years."

"They've just reopened, see?" Sabs held up the ad, which was decorated with a drawing of a horse. "And they're offering a discount on lessons. They're really cheap."

"So?" Al asked.

"We could all take riding lessons together." Sabs's eyes were wide with enthusiasm. "We could learn to ride and jump and . . . well, whatever else you do on a horse. You know — like in those commercials where people are always riding along the beach on a beautiful palomino with a long flowing mane, galloping along through the crashing surf . . . ."

"We're in Minnesota," I pointed out. "We don't

have any surf to crash through."

"We have woods and hills," Sabs said. "Plus we have lots of lakes. You could ride through the woods to a beautiful lake." She sighed.

"I don't think I like horses," Al said, shaking her head doubtfully.

"How can you not like horses?" Sabs asked. "I mean, you're an Indian. I thought Indians practically lived on their horses in the old days."

"I'm Chippewa," Al said. "You're thinking of Plains Indians, like Sioux and Cheyenne. We Chippewa were mostly into canoes. Actually, it was the European colonists who first brought horses to America. Before that, Native Americans mostly walked, or traveled by canoe. During the winter some of them used dogsleds." Al is always full of information like that. She loves to read.

"How about you, Katie?" Sabs demanded. "Wouldn't you like to take riding lessons with me?"

Katie shrugged. "I think it could be fun. But I don't have the time right now, with hockey practice."

"I thought the season was over," Sabs said.

"The official season ended, but we have a post-season exhibition game against Widmere coming up soon. We do it every year, for charity, and there's a really big rivalry between the two schools. The practice schedule is intense."

"Excuses, excuses," Sabs said, rolling her eyes. "Okay, Randy, it's up to you. I know horseback riding is kind of a 'country' thing to do, but it would be fun."

"Randy Zak on a horse?" Katie said, laughing. "Randy Zak, formerly of New York City, on a horse? *That* I would like to see."

I noticed Al smiling, too, like it was a funny idea. "I wonder if they ride English or Western," I said. "Personally, I like English. It's more challenging. Western saddles are too easy to stay on. Besides, they're so heavy when you have to lug them back and forth." I gazed around the table and was pleased to see the surprised looks on my friends' faces.

"Since when do you know anything about horses?" Katie asked.

I gave a casual shrug. "I used to ride in Central Park with my dad. You can rent horses, and there are all sorts of bridle paths in the park."

"Right in the middle of the city?" Sabs asked.

"Yes, but the park is so big you don't feel like you're in the middle of the city. It almost seems like the countryside."

"So you'll take lessons with me?" Sabs asked. She paused. "Well, I guess you already know how to ride. But you could help me learn, and then we could go riding together."

"Not interested," I said, looking away.

"But —" Sabs began.

I shook my head, giving her a very definite look. I was really wishing this discussion would end.

"Well, I want to ride a horse," Sabs said. Our reaction had not worn down her enthusiasm one bit. "It'll be great. Personally, I think you're all just chicken."

"I admit I'm chicken," Al said. "But that's one thing you can't say about Randy!"

I didn't know what to say. Me, afraid of getting up on some dumb old horse? No one would ever believe that. But I was still pretty glad when the Katie changed the conversation back to the English homework and we didn't have to talk about horses anymore.

Chapter Two

I really tore up the sidewalk on my way home from Fitzie's. I had the whole street to myself and I did every skateboard stunt I knew. I even tried out something new — a trick where I jump up and try to spin around and land back on my board, facing forward. Unfortunately, I landed on my rear end three times in a row before I gave up.

Still, at least I wasn't afraid to try. By the time I pulled up in front of our barn, I was tired and pretty sore.

Yes, barn. We live in a converted barn that used to be a home for pigs and cows and I guess whatever other animals hang out on a farm. The farm was sold a few years ago, and houses were built on the fields and pasture. Our barn is sort of separate from the new houses, though. My mother and I have plenty of privacy.

It's *definitely* a change from the plush, super-modern apartment where I used to live in New York City. But I really like it. My bedroom is a loft up above the kitchen area. It's not exactly a huge room, but it is private, plus it's perfect for when I want to play my drums. I'm the drummer for a group called Iron Wombat, so I do a lot of serious jamming up there.

"M, I'm home!" I yelled as soon as I got inside. My friends can never get used to the idea that I call my mom "M" and my dad "D." I don't exactly remember when I started calling my parents those, but it seems like forever.

"I'm up to my elbows in plaster," M called out. "Just a second —"

M came into the kitchen, and sure enough, her arms were layered in white plaster goop. She was wearing her work uniform — paint-splattered overalls and a bandanna tied around her head. See, M is an artist. Mostly she paints, and she's really good at it, but M says you have to experiment with new stuff or you get stale. Every now and then I'll come home and find her doing something strange — like playing with plaster.

"I'd better wash up. This stuff is hardening and I'm starting to feel like a department store mannequin."

M struck a funny pose with her plaster- covered arms up in the air and this spacey mannequin look on her face. We were both laughing as she walked over to the sink.

"You're not going to wash that off in here, are you?" I asked quickly.

"No?" she asked.

"M, if you put plaster down the sink, it'll plug up the pipes. Remember last time?"

"Oh, yeah. You're right. I'll go hose off outside."

M isn't real good about practical things like plumbing. But aside from that, she's a very cool mom.

"How's it going?" I asked.

"Great. I think. I'll let you see it soon and you can decide for yourself. But it's not quite ready yet."

"I understand. Work in progress." Sometimes M likes me to look over her stuff while she's working on it, but other times, especially when it's something experimental, she makes me wait to see the final product before I give her my opinion.

While M went outside to wash up, I dropped my backpack on the table and leaned my skateboard against the wall. Then I put on the teakettle.

I knew M would want a cup of herbal tea, and I could use one, too.

"There," M said, coming back into the kitchen from the yard. "Clean as a whistle and no plumbing nightmares." She wiped her wet hands on a kitchen towel. "So how was your day?"

I shrugged and made a back-and-forth movement with my hand. "So-so. Had a pop quiz in math."

"How did you do?"

"We won't know until tomorrow for sure, but I think I only missed one problem."

"Did you stop off at Fitzie's?"

"Yeah. Sabs got all these little pieces of paper from the bulletin board stuck in her hair. It was pretty funny." I hesitated and looked away.

"And?" M prompted, eyeing me closely. The kettle began to whistle and she lifted it off the burner. She pulled two mugs out of the cupboard and popped in the tea bags.

"And . . . nothing," I said, trying to sound nonchalant. "Except Sabs saw this posters for a stable that's giving discount riding lessons and she got all excited."

M cast me a glance as she poured water into the mugs. "So she's going to take riding lessons?"

14

"Maybe. She really wants all of us to do it together, but Al doesn't want to, and Katie has hockey practice. Some big game is coming up."

M picked up her mug and poked the tea bag with her finger. Now *she* was trying to act nonchalant. "So did you think about taking up riding again?"

"I'm not really all that interested," I said, taking my mug. "I've ridden horses before. I should try new things, not the same old stuff. Isn't that what you're always telling me?."

"I never said you should give up things you like to do," M said softly.

She had me there.

"You used to love riding," M added. "You might find you still like it, if you tried it again. I'd be willing to pay for half the cost of the lessons, if you want to use some of your allowance savings for the rest."

This really wasn't M's usual approach. Normally she didn't try to talk me into things, because she knows how stubborn I can be. "I think I'll go play my drums for a while," I said suddenly.

"Ran," M said quietly.

I turned around and reluctantly looked into her eyes.

"Ran, it's okay, you know. Everyone has some bad experiences in life. What you're feeling is normal. And if you don't want to ride, that's all right, too, and it's nobody else's business. It's just . . . well . . . never mind."

I nodded. She didn't have to finish what she was going to say. It was all right if I didn't want to get back up on a horse. But we both knew I wouldn't be all right until I did.

The next day at school, every time Sabs had tried to talk about horses, either I found something to distract everyone, or we were conveniently interrupted. By lunchtime, I really thought she had given up.

That is, until she pushed her lunch aside and pulled out this huge book. There was a horse on the cover, of course.

"Hey, look what I found in the library this morning," she said, holding her book up for us to see.

"Are you going to eat that orange, Sabs?" I cut in.

Sabs handed over the orange without missing a beat. "It's a really great book about horses. Look at these pictures." She propped up the open book to a full-page photo of big golden horses, prancing in a green meadow. They did look beautiful, but when she glanced at me to check out my reaction, I pretended to be fascinated by my orange.

"Yes, horses are amazing animals. Too bad the only way I'll ever learn about them is from a book." Sabs cast a hopeful glance around the table.

Al groaned. "Not the riding lessons again!"

"The *discount* riding lessons," Sabs corrected.

"Sabs," Al explained patiently, "Katie doesn't have time for lessons, and Randy and I aren't interested in them. If you want to take riding lessons so badly, maybe you should do it by yourself."

"I don't want to take them by myself. I want my three best friends to go with me so that we can all share a wonderful experience that will teach us a lot about life and the meaning of responsibility and is also a good way to meet boys."

"Did you get that from your book?" Al asked suspiciously.

Sabs laughed. "Maybe. Except for the boys part."

"I'll do it," I said.

I couldn't believe the words had come out of my mouth. Honest, I never meant to say them. They just kind of happened. "You will?" Sabs said, reaching across the table to grab my arm.

"You will?" Al echoed doubtfully.

"I —" I hesitated. I could always claim my words had come out wrong. You know, I'd meant to crack a joke like, "I'd do it, but my stamp collectors club is really taking up a lot of my spare time lately." I felt this sort of clutching feeling in my throat, and my heart suddenly seemed to be beating too fast.

"No, what I meant was —" I stopped again.

"Well, is it yes or no, Ran?" Al asked, looking at me strangely.

Meanwhile some voice inside me kept saying, "Tell them no, Randy. Just tell them no." Too bad I hate to be told what to do.

"Yes," I blurted. "Yes."

"Great!" Sabs cried. "This is going to be so incredible! I can't wait. I called the stable last night and found out we can start tomorrow."

"Tomorrow?" My voice came out in a small croak, but Sabs didn't seem to notice.

"I want a golden palomino, like this picture in the book." Sabs held up a photo of a beautiful palomino. Palominos are horses that have a gold-colored coat and either white or silver tails and manes.

I nodded. "The Lone Ranger used to ride a palomino. You know — 'Hi-yo Silver!'?"

"Are they good horses?" Sabs asked eagerly.

"They can be," I replied. "But a horse's color isn't that important. You look for a lot of other things first."

"Like what?" Sabs asked.

"Well, I only took a few lessons and rode a few times in Central Park, so I'm not exactly an expert. But the people that hung around the stables were always talking about pasterns and girths and hocks, and. . . well, other stuff."

"Wow, that all sounds so . . . interesting," Sabs said. She had that dreamy "crashing through the surf" look on her face again.

"Oh, and they also talked an awful lot about shoveling manure," I added.

"Manure?" Sabs repeated.

"You know — what dogs do in the yard that you end up stepping in? Well, horses do it, too. And horses are bigger," I said. "A lot bigger." I could see by her expression that this part of riding had never been in her daydream. Maybe the plain, unglamorous truth would turn her off about the idea and then I could get out of it, too.

But Sabs just shrugged. "The important thing

is getting to ride. Going really fast across a grassy field, with the wind blowing through my hair, then —"

"— then falling off and landing in the mud," Al said.

"Or *worse*," Katie added with giggle.

I must have reacted somehow, but everyone was laughing at Katie's joke and didn't notice. Except for Al. Sometimes I think everything I do or feel is obvious to Al. Anyway, she gave me this curious sidelong look again and said, "You know something? I think I'll try these riding lessons, too. After all, what about my Indian heritage?"

"I thought you said Chippewas didn't ride horses," I reminded her.

Al nodded. "Yes, but that's why I should learn. My people were stuck in canoes and missed out on all the fun stuff. But I don't have to," she pointed out with a grin.

"Come on, Katie," Sabs urged. "You're the only one holding out."

"Gee — now that you're all going to try it, I really *do* wish I could, too. But I really can't miss a single practice with the Widmere game coming up. I'll be going head to head against Barton LeFevre. They call him 'Bad Bart' because he likes

20

to slam opposing players into the boards. Everyone says he's a real animal."

"Isn't that slamming stuff against the rules?" Sabs asked.

Katie gave a wry grin. "Yes, and he'll get a penalty for it, but by then I could be pounded into a pile of slush. He thinks he's just going up against some cute little cupcake. But Bad Bart has a surprise coming."

"*Killer* cupcake?" Al suggested.

"Something like that," Katie agreed, with a laugh.

I laughed, too. But all I could think about was how I'd rather face off against ten Bad Barts, then face up to one single even not-so-bad horse. How did I ever agree to go through with these lessons? Maybe falling off my skateboard too many times had caused a few loose connections in my brain?

Fortunately, the bell rang just then, so I didn't have to figure out the answer to that question.

Chapter Three

"Let's start at the very beginning. This is the front end of the horse, and this is the back end."

So far, so good. Our first riding lesson was turning out to be a breeze. It was Friday afternoon, and Richard Cole, our instructor, had already taken us for a tour of Rolling Hills Stables. There were ten stalls and nine horses. Then Richard led a light brown, fairly old horse named Pumpkin out of his stall on a lead and asked us to gather around for a tour of your basic horse.

Pumpkin stood very still in his spot in front of the stalls, looking very cool about being the demonstration model for Richard's talk.

"He is so cute," Sabs whispered, nudging me in the ribs with her elbow.

I could tell she wasn't talking about Pumpkin. Richard, who was sixteen, was definitely great-looking, in an outdoorsy kind of way. And to top it off, he had a good sense of humor. His parents owned the stables, and he worked there and taught lessons after school.

"You'll be able to recognize the front," Richard continued, "because that's where the head is attached. But there are also two sides to a horse, and it's very important to know the difference." While Richard spoke, Pumpkin was looking us over with his huge brown eyes. He seemed a little bored. "Always approach the horse from the left side. He's been trained to expect you to saddle him and mount him from that side, and if you suddenly show up on his right side, he won't know what is going on."

"The left is called the 'near' side, right? " asked a short blond girl named April.

"That's right," Richard replied. April smiled at him and looked pretty pleased herself.

I recognized April from school. She was in ninth grade. She hadn't wasted any time letting everyone know she was an advanced rider and had only signed up for the class to just brush up on her skills.

There were eight students altogether in our class — Al and Sabs and me, plus two younger girls who looked like sixth-graders and two more ninth-grade guys from Bradley, besides April.

"When do we get to ride?" Sabs asked. I think Sabs was getting a little impatient to have the wind blowing through her hair.

"Well . . . um, Sabrina, right?" Richard asked. Sabrina nodded. "Well, Sabrina, you can ride right now. Just go into the tack room, get one of the English forward-seat saddles and a bridle, then put them on old Pumpkin here. Cinch up the girth, adjust the stirrups and the chin straps, make sure the bit is well seated, and hop on and ride away."

Sabs's jaw kind of dropped open, and she started blushing beet red. Almost anything can make Sabs blush, and she hates it when it happens, so I felt a little sorry for her.

"Don't worry, Sabrina," Richard said kindly. "All this stuff sounds very technical right now, but within a couple of weeks you'll be talking like a real expert." He laughed, a nice, generous-sounding laugh. "Of course, it will take a little longer until you can *ride* like an expert, but I will promise you this — by your next lesson you'll be on your horse, if you pay attention to the basics now. We'll even be having a school show at the end of your lessons so you can show off all you've learned."

Richard went on with more basic horse anatomy, but I started to space out while he was talking about their teeth. My eyes kept returning to a beautiful horse in the end stall. He was jet black, except for a star — that's what you call a white patch on a horse's forehead. And he was definitely looking us over. But I noticed that he also had his ears back a little bit, which is a sign that a horse is not in a good mood. I couldn't help wondering what was bothering him.

"And what is this?" Richard asked. "Um, Randy? Is that your name? I'm sorry. It will take me a little while to get everyone's name down."

I looked up in surprise. "Yeah, Randy," I answered, tearing my eyes away from the black horse.

"Great." Richard smiled at me and pointed to the part of Pumpkin's leg just above the hoof. "What's that called?"

"That's the pastern."

"Very good," Richard said.

"No pastern, no horse." I had heard the horse people around the stables in New York say that. It meant that if the pastern wasn't at the right angle, the horse would have trouble with its legs. The pastern is like a horse's shock absorber.

I admit I was pleased at the look of surprise on

Richard's face. "You've ridden before," he said.

I shrugged nonchalantly. "It was a long time ago, and not really for very long."

"English or Western?"

"English," I said quickly. Basically, there are two styles of riding. English riding means you use a light saddle, and Western means you use one of those big cowboy saddles with a horn. And English style is for jumping and fancy shows they call "dressage." Western is more like working style — roping and all that cowboy stuff.

I felt Sabs dig her elbow into me again. "Teacher's pet," she whispered.

Richard proceeded to show us around the stable and then took us into the tack room. "Tack" is all the stuff you use on a horse, like saddles and bridles and reins, plus all the combs and brushes and things you use to groom a horse. The Rolling Hills tack room was very neat. Saddles hung on wooden rails that stuck out from the wall, with bridles hanging above them from a row of pegs. Other equipment was laid out on shelves.

While Richard explained how important it was to keep all the tack in good shape, I kind of hung back by the door. We were closer to the black horse now, and I was able to get a better look at him. He was getting a better look at me, too.

"Hi," I said.

The horse snorted, tossed his head, and turned away.

"Not very friendly, are you?" I asked. I got the definite impression this horse had snubbed me.

"I see you've met Thunder," Richard said, coming up behind me. "He's the new kid in the stable. When my family reopened Rolling Hills, we had to buy a couple of extra horses. We picked up this guy at a horse auction."

"He sure is a good-looking horse," I said.

"He's a beauty," Richard agreed. "But a problem for us, so far. He likes to do things his own way, if you know what I mean."

I grinned. "Some people say the same thing about me."

"Well, that can be good for a person. But a horse is not much use if it isn't well trained. I'm afraid his previous owners never got him completely under control."

"He's a rebel," I said. "It's in his eyes."

"That's a nice way of putting it," he said to me with a laugh. Then he turned back to the rest of the class and gathered us around Pumpkin again.

"Now we'll go over the basics of grooming.

Grooming your horse isn't exactly fun. Your arms get tired, and, especially on hot days, it can be pretty miserable. But a horse isn't a car or a bike. You can't just park and forget about it. It's a living creature with its own needs. If you're not willing to feed and groom a horse and clean out its stall, then you shouldn't waste time learning how to ride. Anybody who doesn't want to do all the dirty work, speak up now, and we'll give you your money back."

No one said anything, although I'm pretty sure I heard Sabs groan.

For the next fifteen minutes, Richard gave us a demonstration of grooming. He showed us how to secure the horse in crossties, two ropes tied to the horse's head so that he can't decide to run off. And we learned how to use the currycomb and the brush. By the time Richard was done, Pumpkin looked very sleek and pretty pleased with himself. Horses usually love to be groomed. Sometimes they'll even try to turn their heads around and return the favor by scratching your back for you.

"Just one more thing before you go," Richard said. "I'm going to match up each of you with one of our horses. There's eight of you and nine horses, so that works out fine. Our selection ranges from Pumpkin here, who's a wise old guy, very patient and understanding, to Thunder over there. I'm afraid he needs a rider with some experience."

Richard looked over at me, his eyebrows raised in a questioning expression. Startled, I stole a glance at Thunder, then quickly looked down at my feet.

"Sabrina," Richard said, "you need a fairly small horse, so I suggest Bilbo. He's the little chestnut over there."

Sabs went over to Bilbo, who stuck his reddish-brown head over the railing to nuzzle her hand.

"He likes to have his ears scratched," Richard suggested.

Richard went through the rest of the class, matching each girl with a horse. Al got a beautiful bay named Sweetheart. A bay's coat can be anywhere from golden to a dark wood color, but its mane and tail and lower legs have to be black. Sweetheart's coat was a dark tan. Al, with her black hair and tanned complexion, looked like she could have been Sweetheart's human twin.

Finally Richard looked at me. I knew what he was going to ask, and I dreaded it. I edged away so that we wouldn't be standing right beside Sabs or Al.

"Well, looks like we're down to just Thunder and Pumpkin," Richard said. "Thunder could be a handful, but, on the other hand, Pumpkin is kind of predictable, if you know what I mean."

"Predictable" meant boring. Every riding stable has a horse like Pumpkin: an easy horse for nervous beginners, or for little kids and old people. Pumpkin was the kind of horse who knew every trail by heart, and understood the whole routine of the stables so well he could practically run the place.

Richard was challenging me. He had deliberately given away all the other horses because he knew none of the other girls had any experience. I was the only one who could even think about riding Thunder. In a way, it was kind of an honor — an honor I really didn't appreciate.

I gave Thunder a long look. He whinnied and tossed his head, staring right at me with his big, dark eyes.

"I'll take Pumpkin," I murmured.

"Excuse me?" Richard said. His expression was a mixture of surprise and disappointment.

"I . . . I'm a little rusty," I explained with a shrug.

Richard stared at me for a moment, like he wasn't sure if he should try to change my mind. "You're the boss," he said at last.

I patted Pumpkin on the muzzle and deliberately avoided looking at Thunder. I felt like he'd challenged me and I'd chickened out. I didn't want to see him gloat. Dumb, I know. I mean, he was just a horse, after all.

I guess I wasn't hiding my feelings all that well, because I happened to notice Al staring at me. She was petting Sweetheart, but her gaze went to Thunder, then to Pumpkin, and finally to me.

That's the thing about Al. She's always been able to read me really well. Unfortunately, at that moment, I was afraid she could read me *too* well.

Chapter Four

"Okay, which one do you like better?" Katie asked Saturday afternoon at the mall. She was holding up two plaid skirts that I swear were identical. Katie and I don't exactly have the same taste in clothing, although the preppie look definitely works on her.

"The one on the left?" I guessed.

"The one on the right," Sabs said in a very definite tone.

Katie shook her head uncertainly, staring first at one skirt, then at the other. "I don't think either one is really right," she said.

We were standing in the junior section of one of the department stores. Katie and Sabs usually did most of the serious shopping. Al and I came along for fun.

Al's not really into clothes. She looks great in anything, so she doesn't have to worry about it. I'm into clothes, but not the stuff you see in the junior section of mall stores. There are only a few shops in Acorn Falls where I can find anything interesting. When I visit my dad in New York, I have to load up on clothes big time.

"If you're not buying one of those skirts, can we puh-lease go to Cowgirl Blues?" Sabs asked.

Cowgirl Blues is a shop in the mall that specializes in outdoorsy stuff for women. Ski clothes, riding clothes, that kind of thing. Sabs had decided she wanted to look the part the first time she saddled up and rode off into the sunset on old Bilbo.

"I'd really love one of those Western-looking suede jackets with all the fringe," Sabs said longingly. "Or maybe a pair of cowboy boots, like Richard's."

"Those are cool," Katie said. "Let's go."

We headed out of the department store and headed through the mall, toward Cowgirl Blues. Katie and Sabs ran ahead to check out a shoe store that had a big "Half-Price Sale" sign.

Al and I just looked at each other. "Think we should try to catch up with them?" I said.

Al shrugged. "Let's just hang out. I'm about burned out on shopping for today."

"Me too," I said.

"Besides — " Al hesitated and dug her hands

in the front pockets of jeans. "I was wondering if you felt like talking about anything. Privately, I mean."

"What are you talking about?" I asked. Of course, I knew exactly what Al was talking about, but I was hoping she would just drop it.

Or maybe I was hoping she wouldn't drop it. I'm not sure.

"You don't have to tell me if you don't want to," she said at last. Al knows I don't like broadcasting my problems to the world. In fact, I don't much like to talk about them, period. Not even to her.

Al sat down on a bench within a clear view of the shoe store. I sat down next to her.

"You've been acting a little strange lately," Al said gently.

"I'm always a little strange," I said, laughing unconvincingly. "What's new about that?"

"I guess I really mean yesterday, at the stable, you seemed . . . . not yourself."

"Yesterday?" I repeated.

"At the stable."

"At the stable?" I choked. Not exactly intelligent conversation, but I just couldn't think of anything to say.

"Randy, why did you pick Pumpkin instead of Thunder?"

There it was — the question I did not want to hear. "Pumpkin's a nice horse," I said. It wasn't exactly a lie. Pumpkin *was* a nice horse.

"Yes, but you and Thunder. I mean, it's like you were made for each other."

"I barely looked at him," I protested.

"That's not the point," Al said. "Pumpkin's safe and slow and Thunder is rebellious and kind of tough, and you still chose Pumpkin." She shook her head. "That's just not like you."

She definitely had me there. I shrugged. "Maybe I figured I should be unpredictable, you know?"

"Randy, *something* is bothering you, and I think it's something big," Al said softly. "You don't have to tell me, and I won't bug you anymore, but I am your friend, you know."

I sighed. She was looking right at me with her dark, sincere eyes and asking me to trust her. And the truth is, after my mom, Al's probably the person in the world I trust the most. Besides, it wasn't like I had really managed to hide anything from her. She knew something was bugging me.

I looked down at my black leather high-tops

and their purple laces. "I had this accident. A long time ago." I hesitated. Suddenly the memory came back very fresh. "On a horse."

Al didn't say anything. She just waited very patiently for me to go on. All at once I kind of shivered. You know how sometimes you can remember something so clearly that everything — every little detail — comes back to you? Like how cool the day was, and the red and orange colors of the falling leaves, and the fading afternoon sunlight, filtering through the tall trees?

Well, I could remember all that. And I could remember flying through the air, and the amazing quiet right after.

I took a deep breath and tried to shake off the memory. "We were riding in the park, along the bridle path. Me and D. These kids were playing Frisbee in one of the fields. Anyway, the Frisbee went wild and came right at my horse's head. He spooked and took off at about ninety miles an hour. I'd dropped the reins, so I couldn't even try to stop him. I felt like we ran for miles and miles with me just holding on to his mane."

"That must have been frightening," Al said gently.

I tried to grin, but the memory was still too

fresh. "Believe me, a runaway horse can definitely be a wild ride."

"So what happened?"

I wiped my hands on my leggings. "We were coming up to a railing and I figured the horse had to stop, so I was starting to feel more hopeful. But he didn't stop. He jumped. And it was so weird. Like flying. All at once there was no sound of hoofbeats, just this sound of — " I hesitated. I didn't really need to get into every detail. Like what I was hearing as we flew through the air, the horse and I. "It was like flying. Unfortunately, I don't fly all that well. I lost my grip and went sailing off through the air on my own. I crashed into some bushes and went rolling down into a ditch."

"Wow," Al said, her eyes wide.

"I must have hit my head, because when I opened my eyes, I saw all these paramedics and my dad standing over me. Definitely not the best way to wake up."

"Were you hurt?"

"Not really. Some bruises and scrapes."

"That's an amazing story. No wonder you're scared about getting on a horse again."

"I'm not scared," I said hotly. "I agreed to take the riding lessons, didn't I?"

"Ran, it's okay to be scared. I mean, I'm afraid of the dentist. Everybody's afraid of something," Al said.

"Sure, I know that," I said, with a shrug. "But I'm not terrified of horses now, or something dumb like that. I'm just . . . just . . . taking it slow, all right?"

"Randy, if I'd been thrown off a runaway horse and been knocked unconscious, I don't think I'd ever get within miles of one again. Just hearing the story made me scared. The fact that you're willing to try again proves that you're brave."

"Thanks, Al," I said gratefully. I stared down at the toes of my sneakers again. Talking to Al had made me feel a little bit better about the whole thing, even though she had to pry the story out of me.

"There's Sabs and Katie," Al said, looking at the shoe store. She stood up and waved to them.

Katie and Sabs waved back and started walking toward us. They were both carrying shopping bags.

"Listen, Al," I said suddenly as I stood up beside her. "I don't want anyone else to know what I just told you about. Not even Sabs and Katie. Okay?"

Al hesitated. "All right."

"Promise?"

"I promise," Al said.

Just then Katie and Sabs ran up to us, with that excited, satisfied look they get after they've found something great at a sale.

"Check out my new boots, guys," Sabs said, pulling a pair of brown leather cowboy boots out of her shopping bag. "Aren't they great? They're just like Richard's. And I got them at half price."

"Great shopping, Sabs," Al teased. "And Bilbo will be *so* impressed."

"I think he will be, too," Sabs said, admiring her boots some more. "You know how Richard said horses can sense if you're a beginner? Well, when Bilbo sees these boots, he'll know I mean business."

"Sabs — you sound like those boots are magic, or something," Al said.

"You'll *see*," Sabs promised with a mysterious grin. She put her boots back in the shopping bag, and we headed to our favorite pizza place in the mall for lunch.

Sabs's solution for feeling nervous about riding Bilbo was pretty simple. She just bought herself a pair of boots. As we passed the shoe store window, I wished it could be as easy for me. But I knew that buying boots, or a hat, or even a cool, fringed jacket wouldn't make the scared feeling inside me magically disappear. I had to figure out some other way.

Chapter Five

"Heads up!" I yelled as I zoomed through the school lobby Friday morning. "Coming through!"

When I got to my locker, I braked to a stop with my right foot. Luckily, the only teacher who saw me was Mr. Grey, my social studies teacher. Mr. Grey is pretty cool. He did raise his eyebrows and shake his finger at me, but I could tell by his smile that he thought I'd arrived in style.

The whole week, I'd been thinking about the conversation Al and I had at the mall. I'd decided that it was time for me to put my fear of riding to rest for good. Starting with our lesson today, I was going to do exactly that. I'd start out riding Pumpkin, but I wouldn't stop until I could not only ride Thunder, but do it at a full gallop while standing on my head.

That afternoon we headed straight for the stable from school. Sabs was wearing her new cowboy boots and a Western-style denim jacket she had borrowed from her twin brother, Sam. Just as she'd promised, she looked ready for "business" with Bilbo.

"Today we are going to begin by learning how to put on a halter, a saddle, and a bridle," Richard announced as the class started. "And then we'll learn how to mount up."

"Finally we get to actually ride a horse," Sabs whispered.

Al gave me a glance. "I'm not so sure I want to anymore," she whispered.

I had to smile. Knowing Al was worried too, made me feel better about the whole thing myself.

Richard took us all inside the barn and told everyone to stand in front of her horse's stall. Near the end of the barn, a man with gray hair and a big mustache was dropping off a fresh load of hay. "That's my dad," Richard said. We all waved, and Mr. Cole smiled and waved back before heading out the door.

Richard's own horse, Duke, was tied off on in the space outside the stalls that's called the aisle. "Now, you'll notice Duke here is already wearing his halter," Richard began, "but I'm going to take it off and show you how to put it back on again. Basically, you don't want your horse to be out of his stall unless he's wearing a halter and a lead rope. Without a halter, you have no way of controlling your horse."

"Won't they just come if you call them?" April asked.

"Well, April, maybe they will, and then again, maybe they won't," Richard replied. "Horses can be mighty stubborn, and a stubborn horse can make it very hard for you to catch him. You may have noticed these animals are bigger than you are. They're also a lot faster and more powerful."

Richard placed the halter back on Duke's head. Then he tightened up the straps and attached the lead rope. He took the rope and tied it to a rail on one side of the aisle, and then took a second rope and tied it on the opposite side.

"This is called crosstying," he explained. "You do this when you saddle your horse or groom him. It keeps him from wandering off. Putting a saddle on a horse can be pretty frustrating if he decides to move out from under it."

"When do we get to put on the saddles?" Sabs asked. I think she was getting very impatient. Personally, I wasn't in any big rush.

"Right now," Richard said. "Follow me."

Richard led us back to the tack room and gave

each of us a saddle, a bridle, and the rest of the tack we needed.

"These things are so heavy," Sabs complained as we carried our tack back to our stalls. I could barely see her beneath the pile she was carrying, which included a halter, lead rope, saddle, bridle, reins, pads, and brushes. Then Richard showed us how to arrange all our tack carefully, laying it out so it would stay clean and we could quickly find what we needed.

"Now I'd like each of you to go into your horse's stall and try to put on the halter," Richard said. "I'll be coming around to help."

My mouth was a little dry as I stepped into Pumpkin's stall and closed the gate behind me. Until you've stood right beside a horse, you just don't realize how big they are. But the truth was I wasn't scared of being *near* a horse. It was being *on* one that bugged me.

I reminded myself that I'd resolved to get over all that. Besides, Pumpkin wasn't exactly threatening. In fact, he had done all this stuff so many times, I think he could just about have saddled himself. It wasn't like it would have been if I'd been trying to saddle Thunder.

"Now, the halter part was easy, wasn't it?"

Richard asked as the last student finally figured out how to get theirs onto their horse. "The next part isn't so easy. We're going to lead our horses out, just two at a time, because it makes horses nervous when they're all jammed together. Then we're going to cross-tie them and saddle them."

Suddenly there was a familiar scream. "Oww! He's eating my hair!" Sabs cried.

Bilbo obviously wasn't quite as impressed by Sabs's outfit as she had hoped. Richard ran over to the stall and pulled her hair out of Bilbo's mouth, then pushed the horse's head away.

"You shouldn't let him eat your hair, you know," Richard chided. "Horses have very delicate stomachs."

"*Let* him?" Sabs cried. "How can I stop him?"

"You're in charge. You have to remember that, Sabrina," Richard said seriously. "Horses are herd animals. They're used to taking orders from other horses and from humans. But if you permit it, they'll push you around."

Sabs turned back to Bilbo, careful to keep her hair away from his mouth. "You'll be a good horse from now on, won't you?" she asked as she petted his muzzle.

"He'll be good, or he'll be spoiled. It's up to

you," Richard said. "Take Thunder, for example. Looks to me like he got spoiled."

Thunder had stuck his head out of his stall to watch what was going on, and at that very moment he whinnied loudly, and tossed his head. Everyone turned to look at him. I thought I understood what Thunder was telling Richard: *Most horses may like discipline, but I'm different.*

I gave Thunder a wink. I guess I admired his attitude. I've always been on the side of anyone who does things his own way.

Saddling seemed to take forever. Putting on bridles took even longer — except for me and Pumpkin. Like I said, Pumpkin could just about do it himself. He bent his head down so I could slip the bridle up over his head. And he even opened his mouth when it was time for me to slip in the bit. Then, when I had everything in place, he seemed to nod his head as though he was satisfied with the job I'd done.

The other students weren't having such an easy time.

"This is so absolutely gross," Sabs complained. "I mean, you're a nice horse and all, Bilbo, but I really don't want to have your horse slobber all over my hands. No offense."

"Just keep trying. He'll open up," Richard said patiently. "He's testing you to see who's the boss."

"He can be the boss if he wants to," Sabs said. "As long as he lets me ride him."

"You can't ride if you can't get the bit in," Richard pointed out with a grin.

"What if he bites me?" Sabs asked.

"He doesn't have any teeth in that part of his mouth."

Suddenly Bilbo decided to open his mouth, and Sabs slipped the bit in, making a grossed-out face as she did it.

"See," Richard said, "girl wins over horse. It just takes patience and confidence."

It took so long to get everyone saddled up that I was beginning to think there wouldn't be time for actually riding. But no such luck. As each girl finished saddling her horse, she led it outside. Soon we were all standing around outside the barn. It was a cool day. The sun was getting low on the horizon. It suddenly felt a lot like that day in the park.

I realized my heart was starting to beat a little faster. And I was clenching my teeth. It was beginning to dawn on me that it's easy to *say* you're going to get over being afraid of something.

It's a little harder to actually do it.

"Always, always, always mount from the near side," Richard was saying. "And which is the near side?" he asked.

"The horse's left side," Al offered. She's got a great memory.

"Very good," Richard said. "Horses are creatures of habit. They like things to be predictable. They are trained to expect riders to get on from the left, so if you climb on from the right, they freak out. It confuses them."

I double-checked to make sure I was on Pumpkin's near side. Not that he looked like he was even capable of freaking out.

"Okay, now everyone begin by checking the girth to make sure it's tight enough. It will be very embarrassing if it's too loose. Watch me."

I bent down and checked the girth, which is the strap that goes around the horse and holds the saddle on. Pumpkin gave a soft whinny called "nickering." It's a nice kind of sound. I think he was saying the girth was just fine.

"Stand on the left side of your horse, place your left hand on the horse's neck just above the withers, and take a handful of his mane."

We all did as we were told. It was very quiet

except for the horses, some of which were pawing the ground like they were in a hurry to get going.

"Now with your right hand, bend down, grab the stirrup, and stick your left foot in," Richard instructed. He went around and checked everyone's position. "No, Allison, your *left* foot," he corrected when he reached her horse, Whillikers. "Otherwise you'll end up facing backward. Make sure your foot is all the way in, or you'll slip out."

When Richard was satisfied, he told us to take our right hands and grab the cantle, which is the back of the saddle. "Now I want you to spring up lightly and swing your right leg over the horse. Be sure to keep your right leg straight or you'll — "

"Whoa!" Sabrina cried.

I looked over just in time to see Sabs swinging up, as though she were going to get into the saddle. Unfortunately, at about that same instant, Bilbo jumped forward and Sabs slid off. A second later she was on her back in the dirt. Bilbo stared down at her innocently with his huge brown eyes.

Richard hurried over to help Sabs to her feet. "I was *going* to say that you should keep your right leg straight so you don't accidentally kick your horse in the rear and make him jump forward." Richard patted Sabs on the shoulder. "Because then you might just end up in the dirt, like Sabs here."

"He hates me," Sabs said, giving Bilbo a suspicious glare.

"Bilbo?" Richard grinned. "Bilbo's a gentle old fellow. He's just having a little fun."

"Some fun," Sabrina muttered. "Figures I had to get the comedian horse."

"Everyone ready?" Richard asked.

Everyone said yes, although some of the answers weren't exactly enthusiastic. Sabs's fall had made everyone a little nervous. Especially me. It had happened so quickly. Still, I reminded myself, Sabs wasn't exactly hurt — just a little dusty.

I took a deep breath. I could feel my hands shaking a little bit on Pumpkin's neck. If I'd been mounting Thunder, I'm sure he would have noticed that I wasn't exactly in total control. Fortunately, Pumpkin didn't seem to care.

"On the count of three, people," Richard called out. "One —"

I steadied my hands as well as I could. There was no way I was going to chicken out. No way.

"Two —"

But what if Pumpkin wasn't as nice as he

seemed? What if he bolted? Once again I remembered the sensation of weightlessness as I flew through the air. And the faces of the paramedics looking down at me.

"Three!"

I tightened my grip on Pumpkin's mane.

And then I froze. I couldn't do it.

I looked over and saw Al sitting comfortably on Sweetheart's back. Even Sabs was finally on her horse, too. I was the only person still standing there like an idiot.

Then Al leaned over and, in this quiet voice that only I could hear, said, "You don't have to do this, Ran."

I look up at her, but I didn't say anything back. She was right, I didn't *have* to do it. But I *had* to try.

With my brain on autopilot, I just grabbed the stirrup, and swung my leg out and up and over. A second later, I was sitting on Pumpkin's broad back.

When I looked over at Al, she grinned back and gave me a wink.

•　　•　　•　　•

When I got home from school on Monday, I headed straight for the fridge. I grabbed an apple for myself and started munching. Then I called out to M, who was in her studio.

"Hey, M, what happened to the carrots?"

"I thought you bought some yesterday," M called back. One of the nice things about our barn is that it's so far from any other houses — you can scream back and forth without annoying the neighbors.

"I thought I did," I yelled back. "But you put the groceries away." M and I kind of share some of the boring house chores, including food shopping. I don't really mind grocery shopping, especially since M has sometimes come home from the health food store with nothing but banana-flavored tofu. It's not like I want to live on nothing but chocolate and potato chips, but a girl's got to have a *little* junk food now and then.

M appeared, holding a paintbrush up in the air so it wouldn't drip. "Hmm. Did you look in the cupboard?"

"Carrots go in the refrigerator," I pointed out. But sure enough, when I opened the cupboard, there was a bag of carrots right between my Cheerios and M's unsweetened granola.

"Have a sudden craving for a carrot?" M asked.

"I'm heading out to the stable, and I wanted something to feed the horses."

"You don't have a lesson —"

"I know," I interrupted. "I just thought I'd stop by for a few minutes. I don't have much home-work tonight."

"So, I guess things are going well with the rid-ing," M observed.

"Things are going better," I said.

"Want me to drive you?"

"No, I'll skateboard for a while, then walk the rest," I said. I figured it would only take me about twenty minutes to get to Rolling Hills.

When I got to the stable, no one was around. I saw Richard off in one of the far fields driving a beat-up old tractor. I guess he did more work around there than just give riding lessons. Farm kids often have to work afterschool and on week-end to help out their families. I guess they know there's more to life than magazines, candy and videos. I think that's one reason they're usually so easy to get along with. Most of them are not at all what I figured they'd be like when I first moved to Acorn Falls.

I stopped by Pumpkin's stall first and fed him a bite of carrot. He deserved it for being so patient with me, even though he must have known I was scared stiff. He was a sweet old guy, but about as challenging as a teddy bear.

As I checked in with Sweetheart and Bilbo and Whillikers, I kept my eye on Thunder. He was watching me, too, I could tell.

I worked my way toward him very nonchalantly. I know it's dumb, but I didn't want him to think I came there purposely to see him. I knew it would go to his head. That's what happens when you hang around horses too long — you start to believe they're like humans.

When I reached his stall, though, Thunder turned away. Maybe he really had something against me. Or maybe he could just tell I was nervous.

"Hi, Thunder," I said.

Thunder didn't respond. He seemed suddenly fascinated by the walls of his stall.

I reached into my pocket and pulled out a big piece of carrot. "I brought you a snack. Check it out."

He continued to pretend I wasn't there, so I held the carrot out toward him. Thunder turned his head and peered at the carrot. Then he looked at me and turned away.

"Look, you dumb horse, it's a perfectly good carrot." I took a bite and chewed it noisily. "Last chance. If you don't want it, I'll eat it myself."

Slowly I moved closer, holding the carrot out in front of me. I knew Thunder couldn't hurt me. I mean, it wasn't like he could open his stall door, throw me up on his back, and go tearing off through the woods. Still, he made me nervous. Thunder was definitely not Pumpkin. Although he *did* look an awful lot like that horse in New York City.

"You don't like *carrots*? Sorry, but I find it hard to believe you're a horse and you don't like carrots," I told him. "Or maybe it's just *me* you don't like?" Then I had an idea. I balanced the carrot on the railing and stepped away.

Thunder turned around to face me, eyeing the carrot. Still he didn't move.

I decided to give him a little of his own medicine. "Bored with conversation? So am I, " I said and I turned my back on him.

Then I heard him move, and the snuffling sound of his mouth. A moment later, I heard him crunching away on the carrot.

I turned again to face him, but I didn't move any closer. "You don't like taking *anything* from people, do you?" I said. I took a step closer and reached out to pet his muzzle, but Thunder pulled his head away and stepped back. He didn't turn his back on me, though, so I felt like we were making progress.

"Fine, I get it," I said. "It's hard to make friends when you're different. I understand."

I glanced around quickly. I was talking to a horse, and I felt a little silly. I didn't want anyone listening in. Still, know it sounds crazy, but I could swear Thunder was really listening to me.

"See, it's cool, Thunder, if you don't like me right away. Some people don't. Take your time, and we'll like build up to it slowly. Maybe tomorrow I'll bring you another carrot. You can eat it — or not."

Thunder just kept staring at me, but I was beginning to feel like we had an understanding. He wasn't real friendly with everyone he met. Neither was I. He didn't like being told what to do. Neither did I, as any of my teachers could tell you.

No doubt about it, Thunder and I were a lot alike. He had to get over his bad attitude about people. And I had to get past my bad memories about riding. But maybe since we were so much alike, I thought, Thunder and I could be friends, and work out our problems together.

Chapter Six

"Hey, Pumpkin," I called as I headed into his stall. "Long time no see."

It was hard to believe we were already having our fourth lesson. By now we spent most of our time in the pasture or the ring, trying out gaits. So far, we'd walked and trotted. We'd even cantered a little, which is faster than a trot, but not so bumpy.

I glanced over at Thunder and gave him a wink. I'd stopped by the stable a few more times to hang with him. Not only did he take carrots from my hand now, he *expected* them. He actually came to the front of his stall and allowed me the great honor of scratching him behind his ears. We definitely had a good relationship, but I hadn't really mentioned it to anyone else yet, not even Al. I figured it was between Thunder and me.

I saddled up Pumpkin in record time. Then I rode him into the fenced pasture right outside the stable. Sabs was sitting on the white rail fence talking to Richard, who stood on the other side.

"That was fast," Richard said, patting Pumpkin's nose.

"Pumpkin is so easy, he practically saddles himself," I said with a shrug.

"Well, I finally figured out how to get Bilbo to open his mouth for his bit," Sabs said as she hopped off the fence.

"By pressing his mouth where I showed you?" Richard asked.

Sabs shook her head. "I just wave a little bit of my hair under his nose, and presto —"

Richard laughed, but then he saw April on her way into the stable and called out to her.

"I'm afraid Whillikers has thrown a shoe," Richard told April when she walked over to the fence. "He can't be ridden until our next lesson. We'll reshoe him tomorrow. Looks like the only other horse we have available is Thunder." He gave April a doubtful glance.

"I'm not sure if you can handle Thunder, April. You're a good rider, but he's troublesome, even when I ride him."

April shrugged. "I can handle him. I've trained horses for competitions, you know," she said confidently.

April was the best rider in the class — maybe even better than me. Last week, April had even told us that her parents agreed to buy her a horse so she could ride competitively again. There was enough property around her house, she said, to keep a horse stabled right there.

Still, Richard didn't look like he wanted April to ride Thunder. He gave me a questioning glance, lifting his eyebrows. "Maybe we should shift a couple of horses around, April, so someone else could take Thunder out today."

I quickly looked away, tightening my hold on Pumpkin's reins. I knew Richard thought I should take Thunder out. He'd seen me hanging around Thunder's stall. And I had gotten more of my old confidence back. In fact, I'd actually been *thinking* of asking Richard if I could switch to Thunder soon.

But all of a sudden I just froze up. When and *if* I ever rode Thunder, I didn't want a bunch of people around to watch. It would just have to be the two of us. Thunder and I had both made some progress lately. But I knew we weren't quite ready yet.

"Why don't *you* take Thunder, Randy?" Sabs asked.

"It's April's horse that's having trouble," I pointed out. "Pumpkin is fine."

"But you're such a good rider," Sabs persisted. "Wouldn't you have fun riding a more exciting horse?"

"Randy's being loyal to Pumpkin," Al interjected. She had walked Sweetheart out of the stable and led him up to the fence.

"Yeah, I don't want to leave the old guy in the barn," I agreed.

"I can handle Thunder," April said in an annoyed voice. "I don't understand what the problem is, Richard."

"If you think you're up for it, April," Richard said, casting me one last look, "then saddle him up. But I want to warn you, you've got to be firm but don't bully him. He won't put up with it, like old Whillikers over there."

"I know what to do," April said firmly.

Al and I rode our horses around the pasture while we waited for the others to saddle up.

When I saw April riding high on Thunder, I could barely stand to look. It seemed like Thunder was getting over his problem with people, but I still felt I had a way to go getting over my own fear. Thunder didn't even glance at me as he trotted by.

"I finally feel like we're getting to the good parts," Sabs said as she pulled up alongside me on Bilbo. "But my legs and behind still hurt from all that posting." Posting is an up-and-down motion you make when the horse is trotting. The ride's a lot smoother when you do it, but it really gives your legs a workout.

"The first time we posted, I could barely walk," Al agreed as she joined us on Sweetheart. "I felt like I was bow-legged."

I was only halfway listening to them. Mostly I was watching April on Thunder. They were ahead of us by a couple of horse lengths.

"Your reins are way too tight, April," Richard warned her. He was riding beside her, watching her closely. "Give him a little breathing room."

"I . . . I don't want to let him get the upper hand," April said. She kept pulling back on Thunder's reins, and he walked with an uneven gait, tossing his head from side to side and snorting at all of us. He certainly didn't look happy to have April on his back.

"You *have* to be sensitive to him," Richard warned. "That doesn't mean you can't be in control, too."

"Okay," April said nervously. She loosened up on the reins, but only a tiny bit.

Personally, I agreed with Richard. Thunder was different from other horses, and he did need a rider that was sensitive to him. I felt sure Thunder would do better if he had a little more freedom. If I were a horse, that's how I'd feel.

"Guess what I found out?" Sabs whispered.

"What?" I asked.

"Richard doesn't have a girlfriend," Sabs said. "He used to, but they broke up."

"How on earth did you find that out?" Al demanded.

"I have my sources," Sabs said smugly.

I smiled. "He's sixteen, Sabs," I pointed out. "Give it up."

We ambled across the pasture at a leisurely pace, watching April and Thunder. "April looks a little nervous," Al said.

"Hey, speaking of nervous," Sabs said, "do you think Katie's very scared about the hockey game tonight?"

"She seemed pretty calm at lunch today," Al said.

"You never know," I reflected. "Maybe she's just hiding her fear. Sometimes it makes it worse to talk about it."

Al cast me a quizzical look, but before she could say anything, Thunder suddenly bolted, without any warning. One moment he was just a few feet in front of us, and the next he was barreling down the path, running at full speed, his hooves pounding and sending up a dust cloud in their wake.

Without thinking, I urged Pumpkin into a run and went racing after April and Thunder. I only went a few yards before Duke and Richard cut neatly in front of Pumpkin and brought him to a halt.

"Don't chase them. It will only make things worse!" Richard shouted.

"But she could be thrown!" I cried. I could hear April's cries floating back over the field, and Thunder's wild whinny far louder.

"She may be able to get him under control," Richard said, "but if you chase that horse, he'll never stop."

Thunder was already halfway across the pasture, with April crouching low on his back, barely holding on. All at once I saw her slip. Her left foot had come out of the stirrup, and she was slowly sliding off Thunder's left side.

"April, hang on! Don't let go!" Richard cried, clenching his fists in frustration.

All of us sat watching in horror as Thunder began slowly turning around, heading back toward us with April dangling. Suddenly she lost her grip and fell to the ground. Thunder's rear hooves flashed over her, and we heard her cry.

"Randy," Richard said tersely, "ride back to the house and get my dad. Tell him what has happened."

I hesitated, glancing back at Thunder. He was prancing around the field looking pretty pleased with himself. I guess he hadn't gotten over his bad attitude about people, after all.

"Now!" Richard ordered. Leaning over, he slapped Pumpkin on the rear, sending the horse into a quick trot.

I was in total shock. I barely remember the ride to the farmhouse, or knocking on the door and telling Mr. Cole the story.

We drove back out to the field in a beat-up pickup truck, and when we got there, everyone was gathered around April. She looked like she had been crying, but fortunately, she didn't seem to be hurt. Thunder was still trotting around the field in lazy circles, tossing his head, and looking totally unconcerned.

"I am so sorry, April," Richard kept apologizing. "This never should have happened."

Once Mr. Cole was sure April was all right, he insisted on personally driving her home so he could apologize to her parents. April was trying to be cool about the whole thing, but it was easy to see that she was shaken up.

Mr. Cole put his hand on his son's shoulder. "You took a chance letting April ride Thunder, and fortunately she wasn't hurt. But I think this was a warning. We have to get rid of that black."

Richard nodded. "He's unridable without more training, that's for sure."

"No time to mess with him," Mr. Cole said. "All he does is cost us money, and now we've come within an inch of serious trouble." He shook his head sadly. "This settles it, son."

Richard walked over to Thunder, who was now peacefully grazing. He took the horse's reins in his hand and led him toward the barn.

"Do me a favor, Randy, and get Duke for me," he said in a quiet voice.

"Richard," I asked, "what's going to happen

to Thunder?"

"Horses are expensive to feed and care for. We can't keep a horse that can't pay for itself. We're barely making a go of this place as it is." He paused. "We have to sell him, Randy."

•   •   •   •

"Hey, that's not fair!" Sabs cried that night at the hockey rink. It was the big exhibition match between Bradley and Widmere, and so far, Katie had been on the ice the whole game.

"Where's the referee? Is he blind?" Al demanded.

"Penalty! Throw that creep out of the game!" I yelled.

Bad Bart had just tripped Katie with his stick, which is definitely against the rules.

"I'll bet she's furious," Sabs commented.

"Yeah, but what can she do?" I demanded. "The guy is twice her size."

"That Bart is like a *major* big dude," said Arizonna, who was sitting behind us. Arizonna is kind of the California version of me. He just moved to Acorn Falls this year, too. He used to be a total Joe Surfer, but since we don't exactly have surf in Minnesota, I got him into skateboarding. He's *almost* as good as me.

"Poor Katie, she's going to be aching from head to toe," Sabs moaned.

"That creep better look out, or Scottie is going to get him after the game," Al said. Scottie is one of Katie's teammates. She's gone out with him a couple of times.

"Katie would never let Scottie do anything for her. Not even stand up to bullies," I said.

By now Katie was back up on her blades and skating furiously down the ice. The puck flew across the ice toward her, and she caught it with her stick. Then she cut across the ice, evading two opposing players, and went full speed toward the net.

Suddenly she reached her stick back and slapped the puck. It went flying toward the Widmere goaltender. He dropped to his knees to try to block the shot, but the puck sailed past.

The buzzer sounded, signaling a score, and everyone on the Acorn Falls side of the rink was on their feet, cheering their heads off, including me.

Katie took a wide turn and sailed past Bart, flashing him a big smile and saying something we couldn't hear.

"Right on, Katie," I yelled.

"I wonder what she told him?" Sabs asked. Then she grinned. "Or maybe I don't want to know."

"It wasn't 'Have a nice day,'" I agreed.

"That ties the score," Al pointed out.

"You know, this hockey stuff is kind of cool," Arizonna said. "Maybe I'll try it. Those dudes do some awesome moves."

I watched as two players fought over the puck at center ice. Their sticks slapped together noisily, and their skate blades flashed, spraying up bits of ice. Bradley got it, but an instant later Bart stole it away.

"That Bart's a pretty good player," Sabs remarked. "He doesn't really need to be such a jerk."

"Maybe he likes being a jerk," Al offered.

Suddenly Katie came roaring up alongside Bart. With one slice move, she snatched the puck away and passed it to Scottie.

"Look at the expression on his face," Sabs crowed. "He can't believe Katie had the nerve to go after him like that."

"I can't believe it, either," I said. Katie wasn't just standing up to Bart's attacks. She was actually going after him. Maybe she was trying to show him she wasn't scared.

Scottie passed the puck to Katie again, and she sailed down the ice at top speed. Unfortunately, Bart was just a little faster. He veered straight toward her. Katie had two choices: back off or get slammed.

"I can't watch this!" Sabs cried as Bart and Katie collided. Katie slipped and went spinning across the ice to end up in a heap by the boards.

For a second she just lay there, breathing heavily. Bart skated by and said something no one but the two of them could hear.

"I'll bet *that* wasn't 'Have a nice day,' either," Al said dryly.

Slowly Katie climbed to her feet. It was easy to see that she was sore from the way she moved. A new player came skating out from the Bradley bench and tapped Katie on the shoulder.

"The coach is taking her out of the game," Sabs said. "What a relief. I couldn't stand to see her get pounded again."

"She's not going to go," I said. I knew Katie. No way would she let Bart scare her off.

Katie squared her shoulders and shook her head vigorously at the new player. Then she turned toward her coach with this truly stubborn look on her face and shook her head at him, too. The coach frowned. It was definitely against the rules not to get off the ice when a coach said so. I hoped Katie wasn't going to get into big trouble for saying no to the coach. But when Katie had turned away, I noticed he gave a huge grin to his players and clapped his hands. Obviously, Coach Budd knew Katie pretty well.

"Bad Bart had better watch out," Al warned. "Katie's really hot."

A few minutes later, Bart had the puck and was heading straight toward our goal. But Katie was waiting for him. Bart jogged left and Katie matched him, staying straight ahead of him. When he tried to dodge right, Katie was there, too.

She waited calmly as Bart bore down on her. The only way he could score was to go right over Katie, and she wasn't backing down.

An instant later, Bart slammed into Katie at full speed. Both of them went sprawling and skittering across the ice, a tangle of arms and legs and sticks. When they finally came to a stop, Katie was the first on her feet. She leaned over and extended her hand to Bart, offering to help him up.

"Perfect!" I cried. She was probably one big

bruise by now, but she was offering Bart a hand. Not bad.

Not surprisingly, Bart refused her hand. But after that, he didn't go near Katie for the rest of the game.

After the game, we all gathered at Fitzie's to celebrate a three-to-two victory. Even though it was a postseason game, the win was still really important to the team, and the mood in Fitzie's was wild.

"Here's to Katie, also now known as 'the Human Bruise,'" I said, raising my soda in a toast. We all clinked our cans.

"Great game," Al said. "Too bad you'll never walk again."

"Very funny," Katie said, but it was pretty clear that she was happy with herself. "A few aspirins, some heating pads, a couple of weeks of lying around on the couch groaning a lot, and I'll be fine."

"One thing is for sure," Sabs observed. "No one will ever say girls shouldn't be on the hockey team again."

"Except maybe for that Bart guy," I said, laughing. "He may not *ever* want to play against a girl again."

"Well, thanks, you guys, for cheering me on," Katie said. "It means a lot to know all of you were there in the stands. I almost quit at one point, when the coach tried to take me out. Then I thought about all of you." Katie grinned. "Especially you, Randy. I wasn't about to chicken out in front of Ms. Fearless."

I saw Al shoot me a glance and then quickly look away. Fortunately, I didn't have to say anything, because right then we noticed a very large guy looming over our table.

"Hi," Bart said to Katie. "You all right?"

Katie shrugged. "I'll live."

"Me too," Bart replied, rubbing his shoulder. "Good game."

"Yeah, it was pretty good," Katie answered, looking at him doubtfully.

"I have to admit, when I heard that Bradley had a girl on the team, I figured I could just pulverize her and then the team was dead meat."

"I kind of figured that's what you'd thought," Katie said with a nod.

Bart stuck out his hand. Katie paused for a minute, then reached over and shook it.

"See you next time," Bart said as he started to walk away. "We'll win."

Katie laughed. "No way," she called after him.

"He could be cute," Sabs said as she watched Bart walk away. "You know, if he didn't have that caveman look."

"I'm just glad it's all over," Katie said, sighing and slumping in the booth. "I've been worried about this for weeks and now it's finally done."

"So it wasn't as bad as you thought it would be?" Al asked.

"It was bad. *Real* bad . . . but *nothing* could have been as bad I thought it would be," Katie admitted with a laugh. "I didn't tell you guys, but I was even having bad dreams about meeting this big monster on the ice who was about ten feet tall and as wide as the entire rink."

"But you seemed so calm today at lunch. Why didn't you tell us you were so scared?" Sabs said.

"It's hard to admit it, even now. I had built it up to such a big thing in my mind, I couldn't talk about it, even to you guys. I guess I was terrified of looking bad on the ice, going head to head with Bart. But right after Bart slammed me and the coach tried to take me out, I had this flash of inspiration —"

"You decided to take up tennis?" Sabs cut in, making Katie laugh.

"Almost," Katie said with a laugh. "But the major thing was that my worst nightmare had happened . . . and it was no big deal." Katie shrugged and dipped her spoon into her butterscotch sundae.

I dug into my ice cream, too, without saying a word. Katie was truly fearless. Brave enough to stand up to Bad Bart — and to *admit* to all of us just how scared she had been.

Chapter Seven

The morning after the hockey game I set off for the stable on my skateboard. I had hardly rolled out of our driveway when I heard Allison calling me. "Hey, Randy! Wait up."

She was about half a block down the street and ran the rest of the way to my house. It was definitely a surprise visit.

"Hi, Al. What's up?" I asked.

"I thought I'd go out to the stable with you," Al said casually.

"What makes you think I'm heading there?" I asked. I hadn't told anyone where I was planning on going that morning. Not even M.

"Well, where else would you be headed with all those carrots?" Al said.

"Oh, right," I said, looking down at my jacket pockets, where I had stashed about half a bag of carrots.

"Besides, I just had a feeling that after what

Katie did last night at the hockey game, plus, you know . . . what happened with April and Thunder on Friday — " Al shrugged. "I guess I figured you'd go out to the stable, that's all."

I nodded, trying to act very nonchalant.

"Do you mind if I go with you?"

"Of course not," I said.

"Great — because I didn't want to miss it if you're going to try to ride Thunder, " Al said quietly.

"I can't believe they're going to sell him, Al. He's such a great horse." I picked up my skateboard and we started down the street, walking side by side.

"Maybe it's for the best, Ran."

"No way." I shook my head.

Allison looked sad. "You know, sometimes I wish Sabs had never seen that dumb poster for the stable. Things haven't exactly turned out like she'd hoped. I mean, I enjoy riding Sweetheart and all, but it's not some major thing for me, you know?"

"I know," I replied. "And I'm not sure Sabs is even enjoying it much. I don't think it's quite what she had in mind."

"Now it's brought up bad memories for you."

"The funny part is I guess I'm the only one of us who would really enjoy riding. Or at least I used to. Now it's all tied up in my mind with all kinds of other stuff: Thunder, and Katie, and what everyone thinks of me. Mostly what I think of myself."

"Sort of a mess," Al said, nodding.

"Sort of a dumb mess," I said. Suddenly I was tired of worrying about all of it. "This is all stupid. Why should I be so afraid of falling off a horse? April fell off Thunder, and she managed fine. Besides, Thunder and I are pals. He won't throw me."

"So you're going to ride him?" Al asked, sounding a little nervous.

"Absolutely," I said, trying to sound confident. "I'll ride him, it will be no big deal, and then all this will be over and done with."

"Randy, I'm not sure that this is a good idea." said Allison. "April could have been really hurt when she fell off Thunder."

"I know, Al, but it's now or never. I've got to try and ride him."

When we arrived at the stable, I was still feeling pretty fired up. I was tired worrying. I mean, that's just not me. When I have a problem, I deal with it. Maybe my solutions aren't always perfect., but I do what I can, and get on with life.

Still, in the back of my mind I was hoping that Richard would be around the stable so he could stop me from doing something so crazy. Unfortunately, Richard was nowhere to be seen, and his dad's pickup was gone.

When we got to Thunder's stall, I fed him a carrot. We were good buddies now, he and I. He took the carrot right from my hand and let me pet his muzzle.

"Hi, boy, how you doing today?" I asked. "Are you in a good mood?" I wasn't exactly a horse psychologist, but I could tell by now if Thunder was feeling good, or cranky. "How would you like to go out for a ride?"

"Randy, don't you think you should ask Richard if it's okay?" Al suggested.

I shook my head. "I know what he would say. He'd tell me it's too dangerous after what happened to April."

"Don't you think he knows what he's talking about?" Al asked. "I mean, he's ridden for a long time."

"I know Thunder," I said. "April just handled him all wrong. Thunder's a rebel, and the more you try to discipline him, the more he'll fight back. He needs his space. He wants to make his own decisions."

"It sounds like you're describing yourself," Al said softly.

"Maybe so," I agreed, "but I'm still right. Thunder *is* like me. Or at least as much like me as a horse can be."

"How are you going to ride him if he gets to make all the decisions?" Al asked reasonably.

"We'll compromise," I said. "We'll work it out. But if I try to boss him around like April and Richard, then he'll fight back. See? It's simple."

Allison shook her head. "I'm not so sure, Randy."

"I am," I said, trying to sound more confident than I felt. Still, I was pretty sure that Thunder had grown to like me. I mean, what's not to like about a person who brings you carrots, gives you lots of compliments, and scratches those hard-to-reach spots?

"I'm going to saddle him," I said, suddenly in a hurry to get my plan over with.

"Shouldn't you think this over a little more?" Al called out as I ran to the tack room.

"If I think anymore, I'll never do it," I yelled

back.

Thunder turned out to be very easy to saddle. I showed him the saddle and asked if he would mind if I put it on him. Of course, he didn't say anything, but I thought it was a good idea to ask, just the same.

"He looks happy," Al offered as I gently tightened the girth.

"So far, so good," I said. I patted Thunder's flanks. "Would you like to go outside?" I asked.

Thunder responded by walking toward the door. I looked at Al and grinned. "See? We have understand each other."

We paused outside the stable. "Well," I said, trying to sound calm, "I guess it's time."

I stood next to Thunder, holding his reins in my left hand. I didn't want to put any pressure on him. So far he had been very cooperative. Maybe he somehow understood that this was his last chance as much as it was mine.

"Now, Thunder," I said, stroking his neck, "I would like to get up in the saddle, but if you don't want me to, that's cool, too."

"I hope he understands you," Al said.

"I'm not *that* crazy," I said. "I don't believe he really understands what I'm saying. I just want him to get the general idea that he's in charge."

I took a deep breath and grabbed a handful of Thunder's mane. My right hand was shaking as I reached down to hold the stirrup steady and slip my foot into it. "Well, Al, it's been nice knowing you," I said. Al was looking so worried she was worrying me.

I hopped up on my left foot, swung my right leg over, and held my breath.

Thunder didn't move. I let my breath out in a gasp.

"I'm still alive," I said shakily.

"Ran, *please* be careful," Al begged.

"So careful you wouldn't believe it," I agreed. "Okay, Thunder, where would you like to go?"

Thunder didn't seem to want to go anywhere in particular. He took a few steps forward and stopped to sniff at a fence post.

"Have you ridden him enough yet?" Al asked anxiously.

"I'm not sure three or four steps count," I said. I'd actually had the nerve to get up on him, that was something, but not enough for me to be sure I'd gotten over my fear of horses. And not enough to convince Richard that Thunder should be kept.

Thunder began walking toward the gate that

led out to the pasture. When we reached the gate, he stopped and pawed the ground.

"See, he's telling me just what he wants to do," I said.

Al ran over and swung the gate open, and Thunder walked through. "Good boy," I said. "See, Al? He's being just —"

Before I could get out another word, Thunder took off. It was like he just exploded. Desperately I tightened my grip on the reins and hunkered down in the saddle. I tried to yell "Whoa," but my voice was lost in the wind.

Thunder flew at a full gallop while I held on for dear life, terrified of being thrown. Terrified by my memories.

If you've never been on a galloping horse, you just can't imagine how powerful it is. I might as well have been a flea on his back or something. The ground seemed to fly by, just a blur of green. Up ahead I saw the far fence that separated the pasture from a field of wheat. It was getting closer by the second.

"Come on, boy, stop," I begged. "Whoa, whoa." I pulled at the reins, sawing them back and forth, trying to get him to turn so he would slow down. But Thunder kept galloping straight for the fence.

Out of the corner of my eye I glimpsed another horse and rider, but I couldn't tell who it was. Besides, I was a little distracted by the fact that I was scared to death.

Finally, the fence was right in front of us, but Thunder never slowed. Suddenly there was silence. The sound of Thunder's hooves pounding the dirt was gone. We were flying through the air, up and over the fence.

I screamed. Just like I had once before. I screamed, and my right foot slipped out of my stirrup. I just panicked, unable to remember all the things I *should* be doing to stay on Thunder's back.

Suddenly I was by myself, flying through the air. I saw the ground. It seemed like it was jumping up to get me. Then I hit. I rolled twice and stopped face up. Stalks of wheat were matted under me. Dirt was in my mouth.

For a long moment I lay there. It had happened. My worst fear had happened again. I had even screamed. Just like before.

Suddenly I heard my name called. Richard rode up on Duke. He jumped off and rushed over to me. A few moments later Al appeared, winded from running.

I looked up at them from the ground, hovering over me just like the paramedics had. I felt like crying. But then I didn't feel like crying any more.

I spit the dirt out of my mouth. And then the strangest thing happened. I just started giggling.

"Are you all right?" Al asked, her voice frantic and breathless.

"Can you move your feet and your hands?" Richard demanded.

The only answer I could give them was an explosion of laughter. I tried to say something to reassure them, but I was just plain laughing too hard. Then I tried to get up, but my behind was so sore I couldn't budge. Which struck me as funny all over again, so I laughed even harder.

"She's delirious," Richard said. "She must have bumped her head."

Well, *that* was really funny, so now I couldn't get up because I was laughing too hard. Plus, my rear end felt like one big bruise.

"No," I heard Al say, "I think she's fine."

They helped me to my feet, and Al picked some of the wheat stalks out of my hair.

"Great takeoff, but a weak landing," Richard commented dryly. "We're going to have to charge you extra for the flying lessons."

I had finally stopped laughing, but now the two of them were giggling at Richard's joke, which set me off again.

"I like the somersault," Al remarked. "Very acrobatic."

"I did *not* somersault," I protested.

"Oh, yes you did," Richard said. "But it was only a single. You'll have to work on that if you plan to try out for the Olympic gymnastics team."

We all fell silent as we heard a loud whinny, and looked up to see Thunder trotting over toward us through the wheat field.

"Too bad," Richard said, shaking his head. "I'm afraid that's it for Thunder. I'd been hoping that if you could ride him, we'd be able to keep him."

All at once I wasn't laughing anymore. "He's not a bad horse," I said defensively.

Richard nodded in agreement. "He's a beauty. But what we need here are horses that can be ridden by students. Let's face it, even I have a hard time controlling him. I'd love to keep him as my own horse, but I already have Duke, and all our animals have to pay their way." He looked down at his boots. "We just don't have the money to keep horses who can't be used in lessons, and my dad and I don't have the time to work with Thunder."

Thunder stopped right in front of me. He nickered and stuck out his muzzle to be petted. "Great," I said, trying to sound angry, "you launch me into outer space, and then you want to just cuddle up and be friends."

"You two seem to be real pals," Richard said.

"I guess I do kind of like the guy," I admitted, stroking Thunder's flank. "Even though he's nothing but trouble." It gave me a twisting feeling in my stomach to think that I might never see Thunder again. He could be sold to someone who lived clear in the next state.

Before I knew what I was doing, and before either of them had time to object, I grabbed Thunder's mane and swung up onto his back.

. "Randy, are you crazy?" Al cried. "He just threw you!"

Richard didn't say anything. Instead, he just stared at me thoughtfully. "Make him turn left," he instructed after a few seconds.

"I —" I faltered. "I don't think he likes taking orders."

"Tough," Richard said firmly. "He has to learn. And if you are ever going to be any kind of rider, whether it's on Thunder or any other horse, you're going to have to learn to *give* orders."

"But Thunder is different," I protested.

"That may be, Randy. And maybe you do understand him somehow. But in the end, he's either going to learn to be ridden, or he's going to be of no use to anyone. " He crossed his arms over his chest. "So, Randy, make Thunder turn and walk left."

I could see his point. But I had gotten this far in my relationship with Thunder by not ordering him around. Of course, if Mr. Cole had to sell Thunder, there wouldn't be *any* relationship.

I pulled the reins to the left and squeezed my legs against Thunder's thighs, which is how you tell a horse to go forward. To my surprise, Thunder responded immediately and turned a full circle.

I took him around the pasture at an easy gait. I made him stop, turn right, turn left again, and then gallop over to Richard, where I reined him in to a full stop.

"I don't know what came over him," I said in amazement. "He was actually easy to handle."

"Pretty much all he needs is someone who is willing to work with him," Richard said. "Someone who he gets along with."

"I'll come and work with him. After school, a

few hours a week." I just blurted it out, without even thinking.

Richard sighed. "If it was up to me, sure you could. But after what happened with April, there's no way my dad would permit it."

"Oh, no!" I said.

"Sorry, Randy. He'd kill me if he found out you'd been on Thunder this afternoon."

"Sure, I get it." I nodded, trying not to show how disappointed I really felt.

"Well, as long as you're allright, I think I'll just head off now. I have some work to finish. Can you walk Thunder over to his stall?"

"Sure," I said. I swung down off Thunder holding on to the reins in one hand.

The funny thing was I had gone from being practically terrified of riding Thunder to being really disappointed that Richard said I couldn't even ride him back to the stable.

Richard climbed over the fence and whistled for Duke, who was contentedly munching grass.

"Listen, Randy. I know you've gotten attached to Thunder, and you must be feeling pretty low right now. But you tried your best. There's just no way to change my dad's mind."

"I understand. See you tomorrow at the

show," I said.

Richard waved to us and galloped off on Duke. Al and I started back to the stable with Thunder walking behind us.

"Well, this has certainly been an exciting morning," Al said. "Are you sure you feel okay?"

"I feel great," I said. "Amazing, huh? Just like what happened to me in New York. But just like Katie said last night, I'd built it up into such a big thing. It wasn't nearly as awful as I had imagined." I gave her a crooked grin. "I even started screaming like I did back then. It must have sounded awful!"

"I wouldn't call it screaming," Al said, trying not to laugh.

"Well, what would you call it?" I demanded.

"I thought you were just shouting something. You know, like you were saying something really loud."

I gave her a dubious look. "What did it sound like I was saying, then?"

"Well," Al said, "it sounded like you were saying AAAAAAARRRGHH!"

Both of us burst out laughing all over again. Even Thunder gave out a nicker.

"I wish there was something I could do to

change Mr. Cole's mind about selling Thunder," I said.

"It is sad," Al agreed. "But he did throw you, Randy. Just like he did to April."

"True, but I think he's really close to giving up on that stunt," I replied. I reached up and patted Thunder, who was now walking beside me, as calm as could be. "I know this sounds crazy, but Thunder helped me get over my fear about horses, so I want to help him work out his problem about people. I feel like I really owe it to this silly horse."

"It doesn't sound crazy," Al assured me with a smile. "Not for you. But what can you do to change Mr. Cole's mind?"

"I don't know," I admitted honestly. "Maybe Thunder has some ideas." I stopped walking and Thunder stopped, too. I looked up into his eyes and spoke right to him. "So, what do you think, Thunder? Any ideas?"

He just stared at me for the longest moment. Then he tossed his head and made a loud neighing sound. Al and I were so surprised we burst out laughing.

"So, what did he say?" Al asked me.

"He said he doesn't know, but he'll work on it," I translated.

Al just shook her head. "Well, he's lucky somebody understands him so well."

"We're both lucky," I said. And, I knew that between Thunder and me, we'd figure out some way to change Mr. Cole's mind.

Chapter Eight

Randy calls Allison.

ALLISON: Hello?

RANDY: Hi, Al. It's me.

ALLISON: Hi, Ran. How do you feel?

RANDY: I'm still a little sore from this morn-ing, but I feel great. It's like there's this huge thing I don't have to worry about anymore.

ALLISON: Great. So, what are you up to? Sitting around on ice packs?

RANDY: Yeah, and it's getting pretty boring. M went to the video store for me and rented a bunch of horse movies.

ALLISON: Neat idea. They should really get you psyched for the show tomor-row.

RANDY: I can't get psyched alone. I thought you guys could all come over and hang. We'll get some pizza.

ALLISON:	Gee, I'll have to check my busy social calendar. Hmm. *(Pauses.)* Hmmm — amazing! I'm free!
RANDY:	Great. I'll call Sabs and Katie.
ALLISON:	Okay, I'll be there in an hour.
RANDY:	Perfect.
ALLISON:	Bye.
RANDY:	Wait!
ALLISON:	What?
RANDY:	Thanks.
ALLISON:	For what?
RANDY:	For . . . you know.
ALLISON:	Hey, no prob. What are friends for?

Randy calls Sabs.

MRS. WELLS:	You've reached the Wells Lunatic Asylum.
RANDY:	Hi, Mrs. Wells. It's Randy Zak.
MRS. WELLS:	Thank goodness. Sabrina and Sam have been fighting all afternoon.
RANDY:	What about?
MRS. WELLS:	Since when do they need a reason? Something to do with the TV

	remote control.
RANDY:	Well, I wanted to invite Sabs over to my house for some videos.
MRS. WELLS:	*(Laughs.)* What a nice, sweet girl you are, Randy. Would you take her brother, too? No, I guess I'm pushing my luck. Hang on, I'll get her.
SABRINA:	Randy, how can Sam possibly be my twin when he is so immature? You would not believe —
RANDY:	Sure I would.
SABRINA:	I hope you're calling because you have a great excuse to get me out of the house AND AWAY FROM MY ANNOYING BROTHER!
RANDY:	I suppose he heard that?
SABRINA:	Maybe.
RANDY:	How about pizza and videos at my house?
SABRINA:	I'm on my way.
RANDY:	Great, see you later.

Randy calls Katie.

KATIE:	Beauvais and Campbell Residence.
RANDY:	Hey, Katie, it's Randy. Are you

	doing anything tonight?
KATIE:	Uh, well, not if you don't count cleaning out my clothes closet, starting a science report, watching TV, and washing my hair.
RANDY:	*(Laughs.)* So you're not doing anything?
KATIE:	You got it.
RANDY:	How about pizza and videos at my place?
KATIE:	Great! What did you get?
RANDY:	Horse movies. A huge pile of them.
KATIE:	Sounds like fun. Any dress code? Boots, or cowboy hats, or something like that?
RANDY:	Horsey fashions are optional.
KATIE:	I'll be there.
RANDY:	Later.

Chapter Nine

"Okay, guys, the pizza has officially arrived," I announced, carrying the boxes into the kitchen. I set them down on the table and flipped open the lids. "Pepperoni and vegetarian."

My friends were all sitting around the kitchen table, but nobody was exactly paying attention. Sabs was braiding Katie's hair, and Al was paging through one of M's art magazines.

I had already told Katie and Sabs about riding Thunder. They both thought it was crazy to try to ride him, but they did seem pretty impressed. They thought it was just another one of my dare-devil stunts. Of course, only Al knew what it had really meant to me.

"And, for the movie," I continued, describing the rest of the menu, "we have popcorn, corn chips, potato chips, and all the sodas you can drink."

"I hope you have diet sodas?" Sabs asked,

looking up from working in Katie's hair.

"Yes, we even have some of your disgusting diet sodas," I said.

"This pizza looks great." Al took a slice of veggie and put it on her plate.

"What movies are we going to see?" Katie asked. Her braid was only half-done, but the pizza smell had gotten to both her and Sabs. They gave up the new hairdo in favor of eating.

I picked up the videos M had rented. "*Black Beauty*," I read, waving the first tape in the air, "*National Velvet, The Black Stallion, The Return of the Black Stallion.*"

"How about *National Velvet*?" Al asked. "That has a lot about horse shows and it will help us get psyched for tomorrow. "

"I don't know about you guys, but I'm a little nervous," Sabs said as she picked some of the cheese off her pizza with her fork. She was always on a diet, even though she didn't really need it. "I just want to get through that show without looking like a total dweeb on horse-back. After that, I'll probably just go riding every now and then."

"You're not going to keep riding?" Al asked. "You were the one who got us into this."

"I know," Sabs said with a shrug. "But I guess it isn't quite what I imagined. I mean, you have to brush the horse before you can put his saddle on, and then you have to currycomb and brush him after you get to ride him. I'm starting to feel like a horsehair stylist or something. *Plus* there's keeping the tack clean and lugging saddles around and feeding the horses and all. I thought it would be mostly riding around, with —"

"— with the wind blowing in your hair?" Al said, finishing her sentence.

Sabs laughed good-naturedly. "To tell you the truth, I'm pretty tired of smelling like hay and horse manure."

"I know what you mean," Al said. "I'd like to keep riding, but only now and then."

"Will you'll stick with it, Randy?" Sabs asked. "It would be great if you could ride Thunder now, instead of Pumpkin."

"It would be great. But I doubt it could happen. Richard said his dad is determined to sell Thunder and he definitely doesn't want anyone riding that horse."

"Well, I know you're going to blow everyone away at the school show tomorrow."

"I'll be riding Pumpkin at the show," I pointed out. "I could stay home and sleep in and Pumpkin could still do all the moves by himself."

"Too bad you can't ride the other horse," Katie said. "He does sound more your speed."

"Thunder isn't really ready for a show yet. I'd be lucky if I could just manage to stay on him." I shook my head. "I just wish I could figure the guy out."

"I've figured Bilbo out," Sabs said. "He doesn't like anything about me except my hair, which he wants to eat."

"Maybe you should try wearing a hat," Al suggested as she reached for another slice of pizza.

"A hat?" Sabs paused to consider. "That could work. Maybe one of those English riding hats, you know, the ones that are black velvet and round on top?"

"Uh-oh," Al warned. "I feel a shopping trip coming on."

But I wasn't paying much attention to the conversation. I was still thinking about Thunder, remembering how easy he had been to control — *after* he had thrown me. I had the strangest feeling that an answer to everything was staring me right in the face — if only I could manage to figure it out.

•　　•　　•　　•

"RANDY!"

I happened to glance up or I never would have heard M yelling, even though she was standing right there in my bedroom doorway. I was playing my drums, and when I get going big time, I make enough noise to blow out the windows. M is really cool about the noise level, though. She says it actually *helps* her concentrate.

"Hey, M." I stopped and put down my sticks. "What's up?" I asked breathlessly.

"Isn't it time for you to get ready to go to the stables?" M asked. She twirled around, showing me her outfit — a brown suede skirt with matching boots and matching tweed blazer. She was also wearing this great hat, with a wide, floppy brim."I'm all ready."

"Very nice," I remarked. "Very horsey." M has two basic styles: when she's working, she wears painted-up sweats, and when she goes out, she dresses in these awesome designer outfits.

"Well, what's keeping you?"

I shrugged. "I was kind of hyper. I had to get rid of some excess energy," I said. M understood my feelings about drumming. Jamming on the drums is my way of working through problems, or loosening up for something. Sometimes I think if I didn't get a chance to play drums every day, I would explode.

"Well, get in gear. I'm looking forward to seeing you put Pumpkin through his paces."

"I hope you're not expecting anything too exciting," I said with a laugh. "I could fall asleep in the saddle and Pumpkin wouldn't miss a move."

M laughed. "Well, it's too bad Thunder is such a problem. He sounds magnificent."

"He is," I agreed enthusiastically. I had told M about Thunder, even about how he threw me yesterday. She was pretty cool about it, after I made it perfectly clear that I wasn't hurt. She was really happy I had finally gotten over my fear about riding.

"Thunder is just not quite the show type," I added. "Too hyper."

"Too bad. Maybe you should teach him to play the drums," M joked.

Suddenly my jaw dropped open. "M, you're brilliant!"

"I know that, but why do you think so?"

"The other day after Thunder threw me off, he was fine. But it wasn't because he threw me.

He just needed to run. Once he ran he was ready to be nice."

"Like you, after you play drums," M said.

"Thunder just needs to jam!" I said excitedly. "He needs to blow off steam."

"What?" M asked. I could see she didn't exactly get it.

"Never mind." I jumped off my stool and headed for the shower. "I think it's showtime!" I gleefully announced.

Later that morning, when we got to the stable, I ran over to the barn and M headed for the seats set up for spectators at the show ring. My friends were all there in the barn already, saddling up their horses. Katie was there, too.

"There you are," Al said to me, standing at the front of Sweetheart's stall. "We almost thought you weren't coming."

"I lost track of time this morning playing the drums. But I also got a real brainstorm."

Al just gave me a look. I could tell she knew exactly what I was talking about — and also knew that the least said on the topic, the better.

"Richard told us to saddle the horses and in what order to come out into the ring. He said if you got here on time, you would be taking

Pumpkin out last."

"Perfect," I said and headed for the tack room to get a saddle and some gear. On the way, I saw Katie and Sabs hanging out in front of Bilbo's stall.

"Ha! See, he doesn't like my hat!" Sabs said gleefully. On her head was a black riding hat, with all of her curly red hair piled underneath. Bilbo was looking at Sabs as if he didn't quite recognize her.

"Sabs, all he wants is to eat a *little* of your hair. And you have so much," I said.

"Feed him *your* hair, if you want," Sabs replied.

"I think he prefers redheads," I said.

"Do horses really like to eat your hair?" Katie asked. She sounded like she wasn't sure if we were joking or not.

Just then Richard came into the stable with April, and her parents. April brushed right past us, without even saying hello. Instead of going to Whillikers stall, like I expected, she went straight to Thunder.

Richard met my eyes for a moment, then quickly looked away.

"There he is!" April said, standing at

Thunder's stall. "Isn't he a beauty?"

"He's a good-looking horse, honey, but isn't this the one that threw you?"

"Daddy, we've been all through this a million times," April said impatiently. "He just needs some training. Some tough training. Once he learns who's boss, he'll be a great horse," she insisted. "Right Richard."

"He does need to be worked with," Richard reluctantly agreed.

"And you think the horse can be trained so that my daughter can handle him?" April's father asked Richard.

"I do think do, sir," Richard said. "If Thunder is handled properly, he's a great horse to ride." Richard glanced at me a moment, then quickly looked away.

"I don't know, April —" April's father sounded unconvinced.

"You said I could get a horse," April said, crossing her arms over her chest. "One that I can ride in competitions. This horse is perfect. I know I can handle him."

April spoke in that same insistent, confident tone that she'd had right before Thunder had run wild on her. But it seemed to work on her parents,

I noticed. Her father and mother exchanged a glance, and the man threw up his hands. "If this is the horse you want, and I can work out a deal with these people, he's yours."

April squealed and threw her arms around her father. I felt like I'd been kicked in the stomach. Richard must have seen the look on my face because he excused himself and came over to join me.

"I'm sorry, Randy," he whispered after April led Whillikers out of his stall and left with her parents. "April had her folks call my dad about Thunder, and there was nothing I could do about it."

"But — but April is all wrong for Thunder. She has no idea how to handle him. Did you hear what she said? All that 'tough training' stuff?" I said, pausing to swallow the lump in my throat.

"I know what you're saying is true, Randy. But what can we do? My dad figured we were lucky to be able to find a buyer at all. Let's face it, Thunder isn't ready to be used for riding lessons. If he was . . . well, we'd keep him. I'd *make* my dad keep him."

"I understand," I said. But my voice sounded

hollow, even to me. I noticed Al, Sabs, and Katie standing close by, listening. Their faces were almost as sad as mine must have been.

"Well, the show must go on," Richard said, trying to sound more cheerful. "I'll see you in the ring, Randy. You and Pumpkin are on last."

He walked away, pausing only to pat Thunder's muzzle regretfully.

"This isn't fair," Al said.

"Randy, I'm so sorry," Sabs said, putting her hand on my shoulder.

"I'll live," I said grimly. "It's Thunder I'm worried about." I paused. "You guys have to get ready. Don't worry about me."

Sabs started to say something, but Al shook her head. She knew that talk wasn't going to make me feel any better just then.

"I guess I'll head on out to the stands," Katie said awkwardly.

I nodded. It was all I could do right at that point. I didn't really trust myself to talk. Instead, I went over to Thunder's stall and just stood there, stroking his muzzle.

Sabs saddled Bilbo and began walking him toward the show ring. From outside I could hear the sounds of the small crowd of spectator —

mostly families of the students.

The other kids in the class were leading their horses out of the stalls, and talking nervously, but I just stood there, looking at Thunder.

After a while I realized I was all alone. All the others had taken their horse out to the ring, and I could hear clapping and applause. Inside the barn it was just me and Pumpkin and Thunder.

I knew that it was time to take action. I turned to head for the tack room to retrieve my saddle gear.

And as I walked by Thunder's stall, I heard him nicker softly. I stopped and looked at him.

"Are you thinking what I am thinking? I asked him.

Thunder pawed the floor of his stall and tossed his head.

"Okay, if you're up for it, so am I," I answered, heading for the tack room again.

The way Thunder and I figured it, we had nothing to lose. Richard's dad was already going to sell him. The worst that could happen was . . . that I could go flying in front of all those people and look like a total dork.

It definitely seemed like a crazy idea.

But then, sometimes I'm a little crazy.

Chapter Ten

I heard Sabs and Bilbo being announced outside. They were the last horse and rider before I was due to go. I took a deep breath and went into action. I don't think any horse has ever been saddled any faster than Thunder was then..

I led him to the barn door which opened on the side that was hidden from the ring. Then I swung up into his saddle.

"All right, boy," I said. "You want to learn to play the drums? Let's do it." I gave the signal and Thunder took off at a gallop. The gate to the pasture was open and we tore through it at maximum speed.

Thunder ran like it was all he was ever born to do. He ran like the wind, throwing up clods of dirt from his hooves, and making a sound that really did seem like thunder.

I let him go for a few minutes, but I knew time was short, so I turned his head and started back toward the show ring.

"Come on, Thunder," I cried. "I know you just want to party, but we have some work to do."

I looked ahead and saw Sabs patting Bilbo on the neck as she walked him out of the ring.

I urged Thunder on, heading straight for the fence that surrounded the show ring. Nothing like a flashy entrance to get their attention, I thought.

Once again I heard the sudden silence as his hooves lifted off the ground and we sailed over the fence. Somehow I managed to stay in the saddle, although it was kind of a close call. I pulled back on the reins and Thunder responded perfectly, coming to a stop.

I heard applause coming from the people in the stands. Probably they thought this was all part of the show. But then I caught a glimpse of the horrified look on Richard's face.

"All right, Thunder," I whispered. "Show them what you've got. This is *not* a dress rehearsal."

Each rider was supposed to take their horse through the various gaits: walk, trot, canter, and run. Then we were supposed to be able to back him up, turn him around in each direction, and jump a couple of low obstacles.

I figured I'd already taken care of the jumping

requirement by clearing the fence.

I was still nervous about the rest of the moves. I mean, I hadn't even tried to control Thunder for so long. I just had to hope I was right about Thunder: that he just needed to blow off some steam before he got down to taking care of business.

In other words, I had to hope that Thunder was just like me.

•　　　•　　　•　　　•

"I *knew* he was a good horse," April said.

We were all in the stable after the show, grooming our horses. I spun around and saw April approaching, flanked by her parents. My heart sank. I don't know why I'd thought that April might have changed her mind about buying Thunder, or that Richard's dad might have called off the deal. I mean, the truth was that Thunder *was* a beautiful horse. Unfortunately, I'd gotten him to prove just how great he was.

"You were right, as usual," April's dad was saying.

"And just think how much better he'll perform with training," April said. "Not to mention with a better rider."

April didn't even look at me, but I know she

had said that purposely loud enough for me to hear.

"Hello, folks," Mr. Cole said, coming in from outside.

"Ah, Mr. Cole," April's dad said, extending his hand. "I hope you're not going raise that horse's price now, after that display in the ring," he joked.

Mr. Cole shook his head. "Sorry, folks, but Thunder is no longer for sale."

"What do you mean?" April demanded. "I'm going to have him properly trained. He's going to be my horse!"

"Well, it seems we were wrong about Thunder, April," Mr. Cole said calmly. "It looks like he can be ridden. Just needed a little understanding," he added, smiling at me. "I think we'd better hang on to him after all."

"But I can have him trained," April insisted. "I can take him into the regionals. If all you want is more money, my father can —"

"Mr. Cole said Thunder's not for sale," I interrupted. "Besides, Thunder's already planning to be at those regionals. And he's going to win."

You know how sometimes you open your mouth and say something you haven't exactly thought about? Something really dumb?

"Really?" April demanded. "And who is going to ride him?"

"I am," I said. "And Thunder and I will win." Then I realized I was talking about a horse I didn't even own. I quickly glanced over at Mr. Cole. He was still smiling at me, so I figured the whole idea was cool with him. "That is, if Mr. Cole says it's all-right."

"I think it's a fine idea," he said. "Richard can even help you work with Thunder a bit. Can't you, son?"

"It's fine with me," Richard said, looking happier than I'd seen him all day.

"I guess that settles it, then," April snapped. "I'll just have to find another horse for myself, that's all."

"There are plenty of other horses for sale, honey," her father said, patting her shoulder. "Let's get out of here. These people just don't know how to make a good deal."

April just nodded at her father, then turned on her heel and stormed out of the barn, trailing her parents behind her.

"Thanks, Mr. Cole," I said.

"Don't thank me," Mr. Cole replied, nodding toward Richard. "He twisted my arm."

"I nearly fainted when I saw you and Thunder flying over that fence, "Richard confessed. "But he sure looked great out there. How did you get him to respond so well?"

I grinned at my friends. "I just taught him how to play the drums."

"I'm not even going to ask what that's supposed to mean." Richard shook his head and smiled back. "Did you really mean it about taking Thunder to the regionals?"

"Uh —" I hesitated, answering him. When I was face to face with April, it had just come out. As I thought it over now, it did sound a little too ambitious. "Well —"

"Are you kidding?" Katie cut in before I could answer. "I'll bet a month's allowance on Randy."

"Me too," Sabs added. "Except I already spent it on this hat."

"You don't understand, Richard," Al said. "This is Randy Zak we're talking about."

My friends were all grinning at me and I had to grin back. "Does that answer your question?" I asked Richard.

"I just wanted to make sure," Richard said. "You and Thunder are a show-stopping team and I really meant it when I said I'd help you."

"Great — I'm going to need it," I said, feeling a little embarrassed at Richard's praise.

"What about Thunder? Is *he* interested in going to the regionals?" Al asked me with a mischievous glint in her eye.

"I think I can talk him into it," I said with a grin. "He seems to really dig the applause."

"Talk him into it?" Katie echoed in disbelief.

"Sure," I replied with a shrug. "He and I like to negotiate. You know, work things out."

I reached into Thunder's stall and patted his head. He had helped me, and I had done the same for him. Now we had both worked out our problems. I felt good that I hadn't let him down. We really did have an understanding.

Like Richard had said, we were a show-stopping team. And I had a feeling that this was just the first show of many for me and Thunder.

TALK BACK!
TELL US WHAT YOU THINK ABOUT
GIRL TALK BOOKS

Name _____

Address _____

City _____ State _____ Zip_____

Birth Day _____ Mo._____ Year _____

Telephone Number (____)_____

1) Did you like this GIRL TALK book?

Check one: YES_____ NO_____

2) Would you buy another Girl Talk book?

Check one: YES_____ NO_____

If you like GIRL TALK books, please answer questions 3-5;
otherwise go directly to question 6

3) What do you like most about GIRL TALK books?

Check one: Characters_____ Situations_____
            Telephone Talk_____Other_____

4) Who is your favorite GIRL TALK character?

Check one: Sabrina_____ Katie_____ Randy_____
Allison_____ Stacy_____ Other (give name) _____

5) Who is your *least* favorite character?
_____

6) Where did you buy this GIRL TALK book?

Check one: Book store____Toy store____Discount store____
Grocery store___Supermarket___Other (give name)_____

Please turn over to continue survey.

7) How many GIRL TALK books have you read?
Check one: 0_____   1 to 2_____   3 to 4 _____   5 or more_____

8) In what type of store would you look for GIRL TALK books?
Book store_____Toy store_____Discount store_____
Grocery store_____Supermarket_____Other (give name)_____

9) Which type of store you would visit most often if you wanted to buy a GIRL TALK book.
Check *only* one: Book store_____Toy store_____
Discount store_____Grocery store_____Supermarket_____
Other (give name)_____

10) How many books do you read in a month?
Check one: 0_____   1 to 2_____   3 to 4 _____   5 or more_____

11) Do you read any of these books?
Check those you have read:
The Babysitters Club_____   Nancy Drew_____
Pen Pals_____   Sweet Valley High _____
Sweet Valley Twins_____Gymnasts_____

12) Where do you shop most often to buy these books?
Check one: Book store_____Toy store_____
Discount store_____Grocery store_____Supermarket_____
Other (give name)_____

13) What other kinds of books do you read most often?
_____

14) What would you like to read more about in GIRL TALK?
_____
_____

Send completed form to :
GIRL TALK Survey Western Publishing Company, Inc.
1220 Mound Avenue, Mail Station #85
Racine, Wisconsin 53404 Survey 3

LOOK FOR THE AWESOME GIRL TALK BOOKS IN A STORE NEAR YOU!

Fiction

#1 WELCOME TO JUNIOR HIGH!
#2 FACE-OFF!
#3 THE NEW YOU
#4 REBEL, REBEL
#5 IT'S ALL IN THE STARS
#6 THE GHOST OF EAGLE MOUNTAIN
#7 ODD COUPLE
#8 STEALING THE SHOW
#9 PEER PRESSURE
#10 FALLING IN LIKE
#11 MIXED FEELINGS
#12 DRUMMER GIRL
#13 THE WINNING TEAM
#14 EARTH ALERT!
#15 ON THE AIR
#16 HERE COMES THE BRIDE
#17 STAR QUALITY
#18 KEEPING THE BEAT
#19 FAMILY AFFAIR
#20 ROCKIN' CLASS TRIP
#21 BABY TALK
#22 PROBLEM DAD
#23 HOUSE PARTY
#24 COUSINS
#25 HORSE FEVER

Nonfiction

ASK ALLIE 101 answers to your questions about boys, friends, family, and school!

YOUR PERSONALITY QUIZ Fun, easy quizzes to help you discover the real you!

Chapter One

"Hey, Allison," one of my best friends, Randy Zak, called out. "Where do you want these?" she asked, dragging a large biodegradable garbage bag filled with soda cans behind her.

"Take them over to Katie so she can count them," I said.

"What about these newspapers?" asked Sabrina, indicating the piles of paper on the floor.

"Well, first they have to be sorted, and then we can start tying them into bundles," I told her as I pulled a crate of empty bottles across the room. "We have to make sure there's nothing in there but newspapers. That means taking out all the magazines and advertising circulars that are printed on glossy paper."

It was Monday afternoon, and my three best friends, Katie Campbell, Randy Zak, and Sabrina Wells, were helping me with Bradley Junior

1

High's first recycling drive. There were about six other kids in the gymnasium along with us. We are all members of S.A.F.E., which stands for Student Action for the Environment. It 's a environmental club and the recycling drive was our first big project.

I first began to realize that Bradley needed a group like S.A.F.E. after I had helped organize an Earth Alert Fair at school a while ago. The idea of the fair was to make people more aware of the problems threatening the environment, and in some ways it was a big success. A lot of people came, and everyone definitely had a good time. But after it was over, it seemed like a lot of the kids immediately forgot about recycling and conserving energy. I knew there had to be another way to show the kids at Bradley that saving the planet is something we all need to think about every day of the year — not just on Earth day or for an Earth Day Fair.